TERRY DEARY'S TERRIBLY TRUE SHARK STORIES

SCHOLASTIC

The facts behind these stories are true. However, they have been dramatized to make them into gripping stories, and some of the characters are fictitious.

Scholastic Children's Books,
Euston House, 24 Eversholt Street
London, NW1 1DB

A division of Scholastic Ltd
London ~ New York ~ Toronto ~ Sydney ~ Auckland
Mexico City ~ New Delhi ~ Hong Kong

First published in the UK under the series title *True Stories*
by Scholastic Ltd, 1995
This edition published 2006

10 digit ISBN: 0 439 95021 X
13 digit ISBN: 978 0439 95021 3

Typeset by Contour Typesetters, Southall, London
Printed by Nørhaven Paperback A/S, Denmark

10 9 8 7 6 5 4 3 2 1

CONTENTS

INTRODUCTION

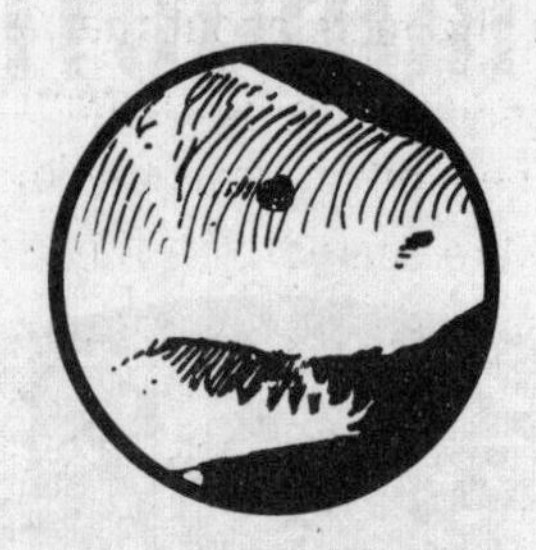

Of all the creatures in all the seas of all the world, there is one that humans fear more than any other.

The shark.

There are larger creatures – like whales. There are more monstrous creatures – like giant squids. There are even more deadly creatures – like the Portuguese man-of-war.

But it is the shark that has the reputation for being the most dangerous. The crushing blow from a whale's tail would kill you – but that seems almost merciful compared with the razor teeth of a grinning shark snapping at your heels.

The reputation for this terror of the seas grew with fictional accounts in books and films in the 1970s and 1980s. *Jaws* was a best-selling book and an even more popular film. The film-goers forgot that the giant shark was "fiction" and they believed everything they saw in the film. Then, "just when you thought it was safe to go back in the water", along came *Jaws II*. More fiction.

But what are the *facts* about sharks? It's fun to be frightened by monster stories, but sooner or later you have to know the other side of the story. The truth.

The stories that follow are all *true*. They are the stories of people who encountered real sharks and lived to tell the tale ...

and you may even find these stories as exciting as fiction.

You will also learn the facts about the ways sharks live ... so you can make sensible decisions about swimming in the seas.

After all, it would be a pity to miss the joy of swimming in the ocean because you were scared by a film starring an inflatable rubber fish! What you need are some true shark facts and true shark stories.

SINGLE COMBAT

There is not a lot to say about a shark biting a human. It is no more interesting than a human biting into an apple. What is fascinating, though, is the behaviour of humans during an attack – the way in which some show true heroism in their determination to hang on to life. It makes us wonder if we would be as brave in the same situation. Situations like the one Brian Rodger found himself in...

Snapper Point, South Australia, March 1961

"Of course you can try to protect yourself against shark attacks. But, like they say in sport and war, the best form of defence is *attack*," the old fisherman said, and he gazed out over the waters of Snapper Point. The sea was too blue to be true, almost like some cheap picture postcard. The sun was already warm in the morning sky.

"A shark has the best weapons – its sheer size, the thick sandpaper skin, the speed, the muscles to lash that killer tail, and – of course – those teeth," he said, and sucked at his pipe.

"What has a human got against those weapons? *Determination*, that's what. The shark's little brain says 'Time to quit' when its prey starts getting rough. The human says, 'I'll be hanged if I'm going to be eaten by some fat fish.' Now a good example of this determination is the case of Brian Rodger.

"You've probably not heard of Brian Rodger nowadays. But back in 1961 he was famous in South Australia. One of the best spear fishermen you could wish to meet. Of course, he had to prove it in competition, didn't he? That's what he was doing down here at Snapper Point – good name for a shark attack place, eh?

"It was the annual Cuda Spear-fishing Club event and Brian was keen to do well. After all, he was the club president. Only twenty-one years old, but fit as an Australian Rules footballer. He'd spent all summer swimming and training. Oh – and that's another rule of survival. *Fitness*. He'd never have survived that Sunday without it.

"Now Brian was going to win the contest that day. There's no doubt about it. Fishing was banned off Snapper Point most of the year. That conserved the fish for the club, of course. They put notices up. Unfortunately, sharks don't read notices ... or if they *do*, they *ignore* them.

"Anyway, Brian Rodger had been fishing for about four hours. He must have swum a few kilometres in that time. He was wearing his wet-suit, of course, and carrying a spear gun. All the fish he caught would have been on a line fastened to his belt. And it would have been a pretty full line, because he'd caught all the common game fish except one – a herring kale. So he headed off for a deep ledge about a kilometre out to sea. Sure enough, he caught a couple of kale and a morwong too. He thought it was going to be his day. It was. But not in the way he expected!

"He was turning back, when he saw a couple of king fish. He thought to himself that this was a bit unusual. You don't see too many king fish around Snapper Point. Then he wondered if he might see a shark. Now remember, he was only twenty-one years old. For all his experience, he still had a lot to learn and a lot to see. But one of the things he desperately wanted to see was a really big shark. And I do mean *big*. Just the week before he'd seen a three-metre whaler shark. Brian wanted to see something bigger. So he took a deep breath through his snorkel tube and set off after the king fish.

"No sooner had he ducked under the water than he felt something grab his leg and shake him. They reckon you don't feel a lot of pain when a shark first grabs you. Takes a while for the shock to let you feel anything. So he twisted round and saw a shark nearly four metres long. But he was seeing it a lot closer than he really wanted.

"And it wasn't a whaler shark, either – it was something much deadlier. A great white shark! Now Brian twisted round and jabbed at the shark's eyes with his left hand. He missed. And, worse, the shark snapped at that arm, and bit it to the bone.

"Maybe the shark hadn't expected this creature to try to poke his eyes out. Maybe it got a shock. Whatever the reason, the shark let go of Brian. That was the spear-fisher's first good break.

"Remember, he was fit, an experienced diver, and *he* was used to hunting fish. The flipper was on the other foot now that he was being hunted, of course, but Brian didn't panic, that was the important thing. The shark was circling round him, looking for the chance to come in and finish him off. Brian was too big to swallow in one go, so the shark needed to cut him into pieces and swallow him that way, you understand.

"That was something in Brian's favour. Still, it *shouldn't* have been a fair contest. The shark was big and powerful. It had the scent of blood in its nostrils and it wanted more. All Brian had was his fishing spear ... and a lot of guts. He turned and faced the shark and waited for the attack. It came a few moments later. Brian raised the fishing spear and brought it down on the shark's head. He missed its eye by a few centimetres, but it wasn't a bad shot. As you've probably heard, sharks don't feel pain and they don't let the odd wound put them off. But the spear-hit stopped this great white. It swerved away and shook the spear out.

"For that moment Brian felt he was winning. He couldn't believe his eyes when the old shark gave a flick of its tail and swam off."

The storyteller paused and pointed out towards a distant reef. "See that reef? That's about a kilometre away ... and that's how far Brian Rodger had to try to swim back. He may have driven off the shark, but his troubles were just beginning. That leg and arm were pouring blood. Even if he could manage to swim, he might die from loss of blood long before he reached the shore. Now you or I would maybe panic, or maybe give up. Not Brian Rodger. He stayed calm. He tested the leg. He could still move it. He remembered his training and knew a tight cord around the top of the leg would stop the blood – a tourniquet, they call it. Trouble is, there aren't a lot of cords out beyond the reef. So what did he do?

"He stripped the rubber grip off the spear gun and twisted it round his leg. He used the handle of his knife to turn the rubber like a tourniquet and tucked it under the bottom of his wet suit jacket to hold it in place. Now he had his one good arm and one leg free to swim back. The biggest drag was his lead belt – he threw that off and he threw away his spear gun, too. That just left him with his float and line chock-full of fish. You know, that line full of fish was the *last thing* he let go! Could hardly bear to part with four hours of sport. In the end, he knew it had to go. He set off on that endless swim to shore.

"You try swimming a kilometre with one arm and one leg, never mind a serious loss of blood. He couldn't breathe through the snorkel so he turned on his back and swam that way. He saw families of sunbathers on the beach and used his precious energy to raise his one good arm and yell, 'Shark!' They didn't hear him. They didn't move.

"But at last a couple of fellow fishermen spotted him, and

paddled out towards him. It was a two-man canoe, you understand. To get Brian into it, one of the fishermen had to get out – into the blood-scented water.

"Would *you* climb into bloody water, knowing there's a shark about? Just goes to show that Brian Rodger wasn't the only spear fisherman with guts that day. The brave guy pushed Brian into his place and swam behind the canoe, pushing it towards the shore.

"When they got into shallow waters, the spear fishermen lifted the boat out of the water and carried Brian in the boat – like a stretcher – over to a waiting ambulance. Of course, the journey to hospital was another thirty-four miles. Took as long as the swim to shore!

"Did he survive?" The storyteller chuckled. "You could say that. He needed seven pints of blood and two hundred stitches, they reckon. But they sewed him up good and proper. Reckon he looked like an old patchwork quilt by the time those quacks had finished with him. Did he ever swim again? What do you think? He was skin-diving in three months. Before the end of the year, he'd set a new depth record of over forty-five metres without air tanks. What a guy! Just goes to show what a fit body and a strong mind can do. Even a shark can't beat that."

The old fisherman stretched and looked at his cold pipe. He knocked it on his wooden leg and limped away.

In the same competition, a spear fisherman called Rod Fox was circled by a great white shark, but escaped unhurt. Two years later he wasn't so lucky. On 8 December 1963, in the same bay, a shark tore flesh on both his arms and punctured a lung. He escaped by kicking at the shark's snout until it gave up, leaving him to be rescued by a fishing boat. Within a year Rod Fox had won the Australian Spear-fishing Championship team event. And who was his team-mate? Brian Rodger, of course!

FACT FILE

Single Combat

1. Each year more people die from a coconut dropping on their heads than die from a shark attack.

2. There are over 400 known species of shark.

3. Sharks are among the oldest surviving creatures on Earth. They evolved before creatures with bones, so their skeletons are made of a soft substance called cartilage.

4. Sharks are found in all the world's oceans except the Antarctic.

5. Some types of shark give birth to living young sharks, others lay eggs in leathery shells.

6. Sharks don't look after their offspring. The baby shark is born and starts looking for food on its own immediately.

7. Shark teeth are always sharp because lost ones are always being replaced – a shark often leaves teeth behind in its victims' wounds. Teeth don't grow from the jaws but from the skin in the shark's mouth. They move forward as they grow bigger and finally replace the worn-out teeth on the edge of the mouth. They are so sharp that the Inuit Indians (Eskimos) of North America used to use sharks' teeth to cut their hair.

FACT FILE

8. Most fish change the depth they swim in by using a "swim-bladder". This is like a balloon that they fill with air when they want to rise, or empty when they want to sink. Sharks have no swim-bladder. They have to use their swimming power to rise or sink. But this is a much faster method of changing levels than the swimbladder method. Of course, this extra speed is vital for hunting. On the other hand, sharks can't float without using their fins. So they can't stop and sleep – if they ever did they would sink.

9. Sharks feel little pain. They keep swimming (and attacking) even when their bodies are being torn apart.

10. Sharks don't *always* get their intended victims. A sea hedgehog inflates itself when swallowed by a shark. It rips a hole through the shark's body and swims away through the gap, killing its predator. A porcupine fish will dig its spines into the shark's throat as it is swallowed. This will choke and kill the shark.

THE REAL "JAWS"

People used to believe that they were safe swimming in the cool waters of the northern half of the Earth. Sharks, they thought, were little-known creatures that only lurked in the warm waters of the south. The people who believed that were in for a very unpleasant shock...

Matawan Creek, North-Eastern USA, July 1916

"I want to tell you about young Lester Sitwell," the teacher said. "It's not a very pleasant story. In fact it will upset you. It upsets me to tell you. But there's a lesson in it for all of us."

The children knew that *something* had happened to their friend Lester Sitwell. Groups of parents had been talking in quiet huddles for the past two days. Their faces were grey with worry. "Don't go near the creek," they had said sternly to the children. When they asked why, they were given slippery answers.

Now the children sat on the floor of the schoolroom in Matawan Town and looked up at their teacher. She was short and round, and wore a long dress with a starched white collar. She had wire-rimmed glasses perched on the end of her nose. Sometimes when she spoke to you she looked over the top of those glasses.

The children knew that Miss Preston didn't tell lies. Not like their parents. Their parents had been lying to them for days now. Yesterday Lester Sitwell was buried and still the grown-ups were lying about Lester.

"He went swimming and had an accident," was all they'd say.

The children always listened to Miss Preston. Today they fixed their eyes on her lips and waited to hear the truth at last. Only one or two let their eyes stray to the old man who sat next to her. He was brown as the pine floor they sat on. His hair was white and tangled. He twisted a faded blue cap in his wiry hands.

"This is Mr Thomas Cotterel ... sorry," the teacher corrected herself, "*Captain* Thomas Cotterel. The Captain will help me with this story."

Fifty pairs of curious eyes turned towards the old man. He just looked unhappily at the cap in his hand.

"The story started two weeks ago, down on the coast at Beach Haven, near Atlantic City," continued Miss Preston. "Have any of you ever been to Beach Haven?"

One of the older boys raised a hand. "I have, ma'am. We went swimming there one summer."

"Lots of people go swimming at Beach Haven. That's what it's famous for, Nick. And while they're on the beach they buy hot dogs and ices and drinks. There's a fair at Beach Haven with rides and stalls and shops. People spend a lot of money at Beach Haven. Now I want you to remember that, because it's one of the lessons we have to learn today."

The old man nodded his head and raised his watery, faded eyes to look at the children.

"Just two weeks ago, on the second of July, a young man went swimming from the beach there. Suddenly he gave a scream and began swimming desperately for the shore. He was screaming all the way. People rushed to the edge of the water and helped to drag him out. They were shocked to see that his leg was bleeding badly. It had been torn to the bone by something very sharp."

In the front row, one of the smaller boys gave a whimper. Miss Preston took off her glasses and glared at him. "Jimmy, your father owns a butcher's shop. You have seen raw meat before. Do not pretend you are scared by a bit of flesh and blood."

Jimmy swallowed hard and said, "No, ma'am."

"As I was saying, the young man was rescued, but he'd lost so much blood that he died in hospital later. Before he died he described how he had been attacked. Attacked by a *shark*. Can anyone tell me what a shark is? Emily?"

"A big fish, ma'am."

"That is correct. It is a very big fish. Now, common sense would tell you that the city council would do something to stop anyone else being hurt. What could they do?"

Several hands were raised. Miss Preston pointed to a boy at the back. "Ma'am," he answered, "they could put signs up warning you not to swim in the sea."

Someone else suggested, "They could send out fishermen to catch the big fish."

A third said, "They could tell everybody what happened. Then no one would go near the place."

Miss Preston looked proudly at the children, then turned to the old sailor. "Very sensible, Captain Cotterel, don't you think?"

"Very," he nodded. "Shame the city council weren't that sensible," he added.

"Indeed," the teacher sighed. "The city council were not as clever as the children of Matawan Creek. They did nothing."

The children gasped. Lucy at the front put a hand up. "Why not, ma'am?"

"They said they didn't believe the shark-attack story. They said sharks only attack people in warm water – in places like Australia." The teacher turned sharply on the boy at the back.

"Where's Australia, Marty?"

"Africa, ma'am?" he replied uncertainly.

Miss Preston looked up to the ceiling for a moment, then shook her head. "Never mind, never mind," she muttered. "As I said, the city council did nothing. But a local businessman offered five hundred dollars to anyone who could prove there had been a shark attack. No one could prove a thing ... and the city council and all the local business people were delighted. Now, here's the problem. *Why* did they refuse to believe there was a shark about?"

The children looked at her blankly. The disappointed teacher sighed again. "Remember I told you everyone goes to Beach Haven to swim. And when they're finished swimming they spend a lot of money down by the beach."

Suddenly the answer dawned on little Lucy. Her hand shot straight into the air. "Ma'am! Ma'am! If no one went swimming, then the business people wouldn't make any money.

Miss Preston looked pleased. Captain Cotterel looked impressed. "Thank you, Lucy. Remember the lesson Pastor Weiss told us last month? 'The love of money is the root of all evil,' he said. Those city councillors *lied* just to protect the business people. They should have been protecting the poor swimmers. You can all guess what happened next ... even Marty."

"Ma'am ... er ... someone else got ate by a shark."

"Eaten, Marty, *eaten*. But yes. You're right. Just four days later, a hotel bellboy was out swimming a few miles up the coast when he started screaming. A woman could see him from the shore, and she said it looked like a red canoe had capsized. Lifeguards got to him in a boat. The poor boy didn't even make it to hospital. Before he died, he said a shark had attacked him. *Now* wouldn't you think the council would do something? But no. What did they say? They said it must have been a giant turtle or a large mackerel fish."

Captain Cotterel cut in for the first time. "They even told the newspapers it was a German submarine from the war over in Europe. Said he'd been cut by a propeller."

"Thank you, Captain, " Miss Preston said. "Would you like to tell the children what happened next?"

The old man leaned forward, eager to tell his part of the tale. "The council sent a small boat to patrol the coast, but that didn't do any good. The shark just swam up river. Twenty miles it swam. Then it reached Matawan Creek!"

Some of the children gasped. A lot of mouths fell open with shock. The old man went on, "I've got a small boat down the creek and I go out fishing from time to time. I was the first person to see that grey fin in the water. Now I've sailed all over the world and I've seen those fins before. Only one creature that's just like that. A shark. What did I do? What would *you* do?"

"Tell the sheriff!" one or two shouted.

"Tell the sheriff. That's just what I did! And did the sheriff believe me? No, he did not. Called me silly old fool and all the names under the sun. Said there was no shark at Beach Haven, and there was definitely no shark at Matawan Creek. Said I was just a lonely old man telling that story to get a bit of attention."

The Captain stopped suddenly, unable to go on.

Miss Preston took over. "That's another lesson from this terrible tragedy," she said quietly. "Don't go calling people liars when you don't know any better. Captain Cotterel here has been all over the world. That sheriff hasn't been outside this state border. Remember, old people have something called experience. Listen to them. How many times have you called a someone a *silly old fool* ... eh, Marty?"

"Lots of times, ma'am..." Then he turned red. "I mean..."

"We know exactly what you mean, young man. Just you think twice before you do it again."

"Yes, ma'am."

Lucy raised her hand. "Miss Preston, you said you'd tell us what happened to Lester."

The teacher looked uncomfortable. She removed her glasses and polished them on a spotted handkerchief. "No one believed Captain Cotterel, so no one posted warning signs down at the creek. Lester went swimming in the creek two days ago. Stanley Fisher was working on the bank, cutting down trees, when he saw Lester disappear under the water and come up hollering. Stanley knew nothing about a shark – the sheriff hadn't bothered to tell anyone. So Stanley went in to rescue Lester. He tried to drag the boy to the side ... then he was attacked too. They got him to hospital. He died. A couple of days later they found Lester's body."

"Of course, the sheriff still didn't act," Captain Cotterel added. "There was a boy who left this school just last year, called John Dunn. You know him."

All of the children nodded. "John went swimming on the very same day the shark killed Lester and Stanley," Miss Preston went on. "He'll live ... but he lost a leg. Four lives lost, another ruined. Four families, heartbroken..."

Then suddenly, a hollow boom rattled the windows of the schoolroom. Some of the children shrieked. The Captain said, "They're exploding dynamite in the creek to scare the shark away. You'll get used to it."

The children went quiet. There seemed to be an empty space in their midst where Lester should have been. The younger children trembled as they thought of the monster that was haunting their creek. It was an image that would creep into their worst nightmares for years to come.

And the older ones sat thinking of Miss Preston's real message to them: the message that Lester's death wasn't just sad – it was needless.

"Please stand," Miss Preston said quietly. "Let us pray..."

A New York fisherman caught a three-metre long shark the next day. It was a great white shark. In its stomach were seven kilos of human bones. One was identified as the shin bone of the bellboy who had died a week earlier.

There were no more attacks at Beach Haven after that.

There were also no more stories about sharks only attacking in warm waters.

A shark attack of the type seen at Beach Haven is rare. That shark seemed to have developed a taste for humans. That is the sort of shark that makes for the most dramatic stories.

The most famous shark attacks in the world have been carried out by plastic models. Millions of people saw the film Jaws. For a long time it was the most successful film ever made. Jaws stars a ruthless monster like the one that killed Lester Sitwell. It also follows the Beach Haven problem of authorities refusing to believe in shark attacks because it is bad for business.

For the making of Jaws, some great white sharks were filmed swimming in the wild, but they could not, of course, be allowed to attack the actors. So three eight-metre models were made. They weighed 1,500 kilos and cost $150,000 (£100,000) each. These great plastic sharks had a nickname – Bruce.

Still, real shark attacks do happen and there are some things to be learned from them...

FACT FILE

The Truth About Shark Attacks

1. The great white shark is the one that most often attacks humans. It is also known as the "man-eater".

2. Other types of shark that attack humans are the oceanic whitetip, the tiger shark, the large hammerhead, the blue, the bull and the mako.

3. Sharks are attracted to the signals given off by wounded fish. They eat the weak and sickly. This may seem cruel, but in fact it keeps the oceans clean. They also follow fishing vessels. Fishermen throw away unwanted fish and the insides of fish that have been gutted. Sharks are the waste-disposal collectors of the oceans.

4. Sharks have large appetites but can go for long periods without food. Occasionally they become involved in "feeding frenzies" where large numbers attack the same bait. They whirl around and tear into the food, but become so excited that they start tearing into each other as well. Their bodies are so flexible that a shark can even tear a chunk out of itself.

5. A study of shark attacks between 1958 and 1972 discovered that of the 1,162 shark-attack victims, only 85 (or 7%) were female. More men may have been swimming than women, but it has been suggested that sharks may be more attracted to the smell of a man.

FACT

FILE

6. There are many examples of people going to the rescue of shark victims and being unharmed. The shark seems to have one victim in mind, and tends to ignore any other swimmer in the area.

7. Shark attacks were reported as long ago as Ancient Greek times. The writer Aristotle described a fish that was almost certainly a shark. However, he said that the sharks have to swim on their backs in order to bite. He was guessing. He guessed wrong.

8. Most sharks will *not* attack humans unless they feel the humans are threatening them. It is useful to know this if you ever come across one when swimming.

9. Graphs have been made of the frequency of shark attacks. They show that most attacks happen at weekends. This is not because sharks are hungrier at the weekend! It is because there are more noisy, splashing swimmers in the sea to attract their attention.

10. A man swimming off the coast of Cornwall in England, in the summer of 1994, was amazed to see his friends waving desperately for him to come ashore. He swam steadily to where they were waiting, stood on the beach and then turned to look at what they were so frantic about. A shark's fin was moving slowly through the water not far from where he had been swimming. The swimmer almost fainted with shock. The locals just laughed. It was a basking shark, they explained. A harmless vegetarian. One of almost 400 shark types...

F
A
C
T

F

Shark Types

1. **The Greenland shark** is so lazy that it's a mystery how it catches any food! It is usually found with a small white shellfish attached to each eyeball. These can make it blind, but some scientists reckon the shellfish lure small fish close enough to the shark's jaws to be eaten.

2. **The hammerhead shark** has a curiously flattened nose with its nostrils on the edge. This makes it the shark with the best sense of smell. It sweeps its head backwards and forwards over the seabed like a metal detector. This way it can sniff out its favourite food – stingrays.

3. **Hammerheads** are as likely to attack other hammerhead sharks as they are to attack humans.

4. **Dwarf sharks** are the smallest sharks but have the longest name. They're called *tsuranagakobitozami* in Japan – all 150 mm of them. The name means "long-faced dwarf shark".

5. **Bull sharks** don't give up easily. They have been known to chase their victims on to dry land.

6. **A thresher shark** will beat its tail to frighten small fish into a large group. This makes it easier to swallow large numbers at once.

7. **Sand sharks** work as a team. They drive their favourite blue fish towards the shore, like sheepdogs herding sheep into a pen. They catch them when the fish can't go any further.

FACT FILE

8. **Sand tiger sharks** are the only creatures that eat one another *before* they are born. The first two that hatch inside the mother eat all the other eggs before they leave the womb.

9. **Tiger sharks** get their name from the fact that they are striped, of course. But zebra sharks are only striped when they are young. In later life the stripes break up into blotches. The zebra shark, in fact, is spotty!

10. **Angel sharks** have large flat fins like the wings of an angel. They were prized by Samurai warriors in Japan. They wrapped the skin of the angel shark around the handles of their swords. The skin was so rough that it created a very good grip, and the sword did not slip when they were using it.

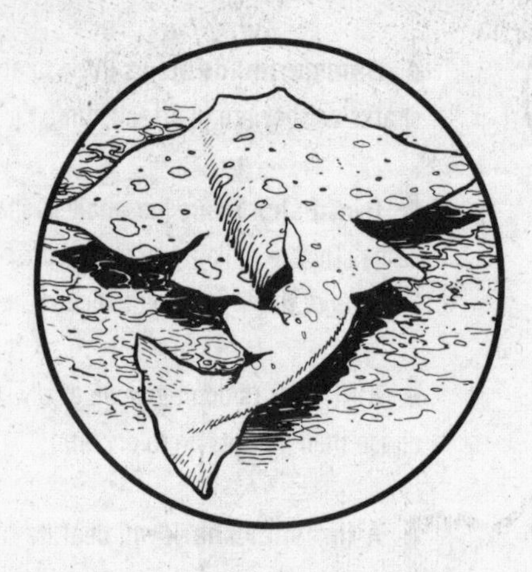

THE SHARK THAT SOLVED A CRIME

There is a famous story of a shark that was caught and put in an Australian marine park in 1935. After a couple of days it was sick and threw up a human arm. But the arm hadn't been chewed off by the shark. It had been cut off cleanly, by a knife. The police had a crime to solve. If it hadn't been for the shark then the crime might never have been detected. But an equally amazing and true story happened over a hundred years before...

Port Royal, the Caribbean, 1799

Lieutenant Huger Wylie rested his elbows on the table and buried his face in his hands.It was a young face, tanned by the sun and the wind of two years at sea.

His sister, Annette, looked at him. She was a little older but had the same fine features. A thin nose, brown eyes set wide apart, a high forehead and a determined chin.

She opened her mouth to speak then closed it again. She had been going to say "Cheer up, Huger," but she knew that it was a useless thing to say at this moment. She thought a while, then said carefully, "Tell me again what the problem is. There must be a way out of it."

The young man stared at the starched white tablecloth. An oil lamp flickered miserably in the centre of the table and its shadows deepened the worried creases in his face. "There's nothing to be done. I made a mistake. It has ruined me ... ruined *us*. I will have to sell the house. Everything."

Annette looked around the room. The furniture was fine and old but not worth a great deal. "I can sell my jewels. The ones mother left me."

Her brother looked up sharply. "No!"

"I never wear them." She shrugged. "There are no young men that I want to impress here in Jamaica."

"Not even George Tilson?" her brother asked, a mischievous tone creeping into his tired voice.

She looked at him sternly. "I do not want to talk about Midshipman Tilson," she snapped. "He is a friend of yours and he is not a good influence, if you ask me. Now, let's go over the problem again."

Huger leaned back and the chair creaked gently. "We are at war with France, Annette. France wants to trade with Jamaica. My job is to stop any French ships reaching this island. Or any ships of their friends, the Americans."

"You are far too young to have such a job," she said.

"Younger men than me are fighting for Admiral Nelson back in Europe!" he replied angrily. "I'm just some sort of ... of gamekeeper trying to catch poachers at sea. It's not real war. It's not dangerous. It's not like fighting for your country."

"Calm down, Huger, and tell me about this ship ... what was it called again?"

"The *Nancy*," he told her.

"Silly name for a ship. Anyway, this *Nancy* is an American ship..."

"Of course," Huger put in dryly. "But, when we stopped her, she said she was a *Dutch* ship."

Annette looked in the mirror above the fireplace and twisted a curl of hair thoughtfully. "The Dutch are not in the war, so you have no right to stop and search a Dutch ship. Is that correct?"

"That is not *quite* correct," her brother sighed. "As I was trying to explain, the French want to trade with Jamaica, so they sometimes use other countries' ships."

"That's cheating," Annette said.

"Exactly," Huger nodded. "My job is to stop any suspicious vessels and search them. If they are working for the French then I arrest them."

"And what made you think *Nancy* was working for the French?" she prompted him.

He rubbed his eyes and tried to think back. "I was sailing round Cape Tiburon in the *Sparrow* –"

"Another stupid name," his sister muttered.

"...and we saw the *Nancy* sailing away from us. I was sure that she changed course when she caught sight of us. She was trying to run away. I clapped on full sail and went after her. At first she ignored all our signals to stop. Pretended she didn't see them. In the end I was forced to fire a shot across her bows to warn her. She could see we were catching her anyway, so she lowered her sails and waited for us to come alongside."

"So they didn't fight you?" Annette asked.

"Lord, no! The *Nancy* hadn't a cannon on board. She's a trading ship. But I could tell they weren't pleased to see us."

"How?"

"Well, the captain was very annoyed. Said he had a valuable cargo that would go rotten if he didn't deliver it quickly. Said he'd lose a thousand pounds if we held him up. He also said he held me responsible for any delay. He threatened to sue me if I'd stopped him without a good reason."

"What a bully," Annette said. "If I'd been there I'd have given him a piece of my mind."

"Just as well you weren't there," Huger said, and managed a small smile. His sister's temper was nearly as bad as his own.

"And you found nothing on board the ship to prove he was working for the French?"

"Nothing," her brother sighed.

"You could have let the captain go," she pointed out.

"I *could*," Huger said slowly. "But there was something wrong about that ship. I decided it would have to come into Port Royal for a proper search."

"And you still found nothing?"

Huger shrugged and the silver buttons on his uniform glinted in the lamplight. "We went to court and the justices could find nothing wrong with the captain's documents. *Dutch* documents. They released him."

"And that should have been the end of it, " Annette said. "You were only doing your job. It wasn't your fault that he was innocent."

"It was *my* fault that he was *stopped*. His cargo went bad while he was waiting to be tried. He's blaming me. He wants two thousand pounds. A thousand for the loss of the cargo and another thousand for the business he's lost by being arrested. It will ruin me, Annette ... ruin us."

"Only if the court finds you were to blame," she said firmly.

"They will," he groaned.

There was a sharp rap on the door, and without waiting for an answer a young seaman walked into the room. "Evening, Annie," he grinned at Annette.

She stuck out her chin and her lips were pressed tightly together. "My name is Annette – but I would prefer it if you would address me as Miss Wylie."

"And my name is Midshipman Tilson ... but you can call me

Georgie. That's what my friends call me, don't they, Huger?"

Huger Wylie nodded his head while his sister glared at the visitor. George Tilson sat at the table without being invited. "Cheer up, Huger, it's not the end of the world, you know."

Annette took a deep breath through her thin nose and said, "Midshipman Tilson, we have already established that it is not the end of the world. In fact I was just assuring my brother of that when we were ... *interrupted*."

"Don't worry, Annie my girl, I am an angel sent from heaven with a miracle to save your baby brother," the sailor smiled.

"Mr Tilson, I would prefer it if you did not refer to the good Lord's angels in that disrespectful manner."

He held up a hand. "Wouldn't normally, Annie my flower, but when you hear my story you will agree that young Huger here has his very own guardian angel up there watching over him."

"I hardly think..."

"Let me finish," George Tilson said more quietly. "My excitement got the better of me. I apologize, Miss Wylie."

She looked down her fine nose. "Apology accepted. Now tell us what the fuss is about. Can you really help Huger?" she asked, and slipped into a chair next to the visitor.

George Tilson had an audience. He looked at the Wylies and began his story. "You were on patrol off the Island of St Domingo when you saw the *Nancy*," he said to Huger. "Now it just happened that yesterday I was in the *same* waters looking for French traders. The wind was slack and we weren't getting anywhere fast. The men were restless and I suggested that they throw a few fishing lines over the side to see if they could catch us a nice fresh supper. But the waters were almost empty of fish. You would not believe it. We caught one funny little red-and-blue striped thing but it was too small to eat. That's when I had a thought."

"Even *you* have to have them once in a while," Annette Wylie said, and her eyes glittered in the lamplight like her brother's silver buttons.

George gave a sniff as if he was hurt by the remark but was trying to ignore it. "I was sure that there was something scaring the fish away from the place..."

"Perhaps they caught sight of you looking over the side, Midshipman Tilson," Annette said.

"My looks have never been known to scare anyone, Miss Wylie," he replied like a shot. "As I was saying, before I was ... *interrupted*, I had a thought that some big fish was scaring the others away. And if we used the red-and-blue fish as bait, then we might just catch that big fish."

Annette was leaning forward now, eager to hear the rest of the tale. "And you did?"

George Tilson leaned back and enjoyed telling the story in his own good time. "We were fishing for an hour. Still nothing but tiddlers. Then one of the men gave a cry. I ran across to him. The line was tight enough to snap. Some monster was dragging him towards the gunwales ... that's the side of the ship, Miss Wylie."

"I know what a gunwale is, Mr Tilson. My father was an admiral," she said frostily.

"Of course," George said, with a small bow of his head. "Where was I?"

"You were at the gunwale with a monster," Annette reminded him.

"Ah, yes. The chap with the line wanted to let go, but I gave him a hand. My strength made all the difference. Together we hauled the creature on to the deck. And what do you think it was?"

"A polar bear, perhaps, Mr Tilson?" the young woman said.

"Something larger – something larger than me! More dangerous than any polar bear on Earth. Teeth like razors and jaws of steel. A tail that was lashing strongly enough to beat a man senseless." The sailor paused for effect. "A shark."

"Is that all?" Annette said wearily. "It can't have been very large or it would have snapped your line," she sniffed.

George Tilson frowned. "It was big enough to give twenty men their supper that night," he said.

Annette Wylie shrugged. "I don't see how your fisherman's tale can help Huger."

The sailor's eager eyes were fixed on hers. "As I was about to say, before I was ... *interrupted*, ten minutes after I'd caught the shark the ship's cook came on deck. 'Stand by to receive letters from home, my boys,' he said. 'The postman's come on board!' And the cook held out a parcel of papers that he'd found stuck in the shark's throat!"

This time even Annette was stunned into silence.

Then George Tilson reached into the inside pocket of his uniform and pulled out a package. He unfolded it on the table. The three leaned forward till their heads were touching. Annette read the first words softly. "*Nancy* – Sailing Orders."

The young sailor nodded eagerly. "And look where the cargo is going to," he said.

Huger Wylie's voice was trembling as he placed his finger against the name. "Le Havre ... France. He was trading with the French after all!"

"Just as you said, Huger," Annette cried.

Huger snatched the papers from the table and ran to the door. "He's about to set sail on the next tide. With these I'll be able to order his arrest! Thanks, Georgie – you've saved my life!" he cried, as he rushed through the door.

"So the captain of *Nancy* threw these over the side when he saw Huger following him," Annette said.

"And the shark swallowed them," George Tilson nodded.

"What a stroke of luck," the young woman said.

"What about my catching the shark?" George objected.

"We should celebrate, Mr Tilson," she said.

"Call me George."

"Could I make you a cup of tea? Or perhaps some wine ... George?"

"Wine would be most acceptable, Miss Wylie."

The young woman reached for a bottle on the sideboard and began filling two crystal glasses. She passed one to her brother's friend. "Call me Annette," she said.

The captain of the Nancy was so shocked at the miraculous discovery of the documents that he admitted everything. Instead of being fined for wrongful arrest, Huger Wylie was given a huge reward of £3,000.

There are many folk tales and legends about fish being caught and strange treasures being found inside them. These old legends are just fiction. However, Huger Wylie's shark story is almost certainly true.

Look at some of these facts about sharks and you may begin to realize just how it was possible...

1. Sharks bite – but they don't chew. They would choke from lack of oxygen if they tried to chew something. The teeth simply hold the prey while the shark tries to swallow it whole or in large pieces. A shark can swallow something half its own size in one gulp. (That's rather like you trying to swallow ten bags of sugar in one go.) A shark grabbing the Nancy's documents would not have torn them.

2. Because sharks will eat almost anything, there have been some strange things found in the stomachs of dead sharks. These include tin cans, tyres – and even shotguns! One shark was found starved to death in 1932. It had a large barrel of fish stuck in its throat. The idea of a shark grabbing a packet of documents is not so unlikely.

3. The stomachs of sharks are especially strong. The juices of a great white shark's stomach are so strong they would blister your skin. But if a pack of papers had not reached the stomach, they would not be damaged.

But it is not only the strange digestion of sharks that makes them unusual...

Did You Know...?

1. No one is sure where the word "shark" came from, though it may be from the German word *schurke*, meaning "a greedy parasite".. A "land shark" in German history was a person who swindled a poor sailor when he came ashore. In our language it has come to mean something (or someone) that swallows greedily. So...

- A *loan-shark* is someone who will lend you money – then take back much, much more.
- In 1960s' slang a *shark* was a student who was out to get all the best marks for him- or herself.

2. One-third of a shark's brain is dedicated to using its sense of smell. It can detect blood in the water up to one kilometre away. It can scent one part of blood in one hundred million parts of water.

3. The flesh of most fish is almost free of natural salt. Doctors tell patients to eat fish if they want a salt-free diet. Yet shark flesh is full of salt – it is as salty as the sea.

4. The carpet shark has growths on its body like plants. Small fish come along to eat the plants – and end up being eaten by the shark.

5. Almost all fish are known as "cold-blooded". But the great

FACT FILE

white shark is one of only four fish considered to be *warm-blooded.*

6. Sharks' eyes glow in the dark like a cat's.

7. Sharks hardly ever eat people in Britain – but people in Britain eat millions of sharks every year! One of Britain's most popular meals is fish and chips; and the sort of fish offered in fish shops today is often "dogfish". And dogfish is a type of shark.

8. Many fish can swim backwards – sharks can't.

9. Male sharks try to attract females with playful but harmless nips. The female on the other hand is not so playful and she can easily kill the male.

10. Shark skin is very rough. If the shark's teeth don't get you, then the rubbing of its body can give you a very nasty graze. Shark skin has been used as a type of sandpaper – it is known as *shagreen.*

A TIME TO DIE

Sharks kill to eat – sometimes they kill to defend themselves. Humans kill for many reasons. They kill animals that they don't eat; they kill some creatures just because they have become a nuisance. If they killed another human who became a nuisance, that would be murder...

Durban, South Africa, Winter 1959

The room was filled with cigarette smoke, blue smoke drifting across the weak, yellow light bulb. Both men had sore and red eyes from the smoke, but neither seemed to notice or care.

It was late, they were tired, and they were clearly very worried.

The smaller one had a weasel face and a straggling moustache. He wore a hat, even though he was in the warm room. It covered his thin, colourless hair. "We have to kill him," he said. His voice was hoarse and strained. The badge on his dark-blue overall said, "Assistant Director – Henry Boetz".

The other man had a wild bush of white hair over a red face. "Murder," he muttered. His badge said, "Director – Dave Davidson."

"Murder," Boetz agreed. "I'm not scared to use the word. Murder. We got to murder Willie."

"He's a good friend, Willie," Davidson said.

"All good friends come to an end," Boetz snarled.

"But Willie's made us a lot of money," the Director reminded his assistant.

The little man sniffed loudly through his long, thin nose. "He's cost us a lot of money too."

Davidson nodded unhappily. "If we're going to do it ... if we're going to murder Willie, we got to make sure we get away with it."

"Of course."

"We don't want to be accused of arranging his death."

"Agreed."

"So we have to make it look like an accident."

"Or natural causes," Boetz added.

"Which is it to be? Accident or natural causes?"

Boetz scratched his chin with a thin, nicotine-stained finger. He reached for the cigarette packet on the table. He shook it. The packet was empty. "Natural causes – we'll get away with it. Everybody knows Willie's our best pal. No one would ever suspect us of ... murder."

"How do we do it?" Davidson asked.

"Suffocate him. That won't leave any marks," Boetz said.

Davidson nodded his heavy head. "When do we do it?"

"Tonight," the little weasel-faced man answered immediately. "Tonight we kill him. Tomorrow we announce the death. We say we found poor Willie dead when we called him for breakfast."

Davidson lifted his hand a little way off the table. It was shaking. Boetz looked him in the eye. "Scared?" he asked.

"Aren't you?" the Director replied.

"Not scared of being caught," his assistant said. "I'm scared of Willie. He's a big guy. Have you ever thought that he might just get us first?"

"Come *on*!" Davidson said. "We're just scaring ourselves.

Remember, we're smarter than him."

"But he's bigger than us ... bigger than both of us put together!" Boetz whined.

Davidson thumped the table. "When it comes down to it, we are *men*. Willie's just a *shark*. Let's do it."

The reporter was young and fresh-faced. She coughed as she stepped into the stale smoke of Davidson's office the next morning. "Kathy Miller," she said brightly. "*Durban Evening News*. Could I have an interview, Mr Davidson?"

"Why?" the white-haired man said carefully.

"Why ... about the death of Willie, Mr Davidson. He's one of the best-loved characters in Durban. His death is the biggest news since the mayor's wig fell in the soup at the council party ... in fact he's a greater loss to the people than the mayor's wig ever was. The people really loved Willie."

Davidson scowled, but Boetz stepped from his shadow and said, "And we did too, Miss Miller. Loved that shark like he was our brother."

"So you must be upset by his sudden death?" she asked, and quickly pulled a notepad and pencil from her shoulder bag.

"Cried like a baby, didn't you, Mr Davidson?" Boetz said.

"Like a baby," Davidson agreed. "Er ... come in ... take a seat, Miss Mills."

"Miller, Kathy Miller."

"Whatever," Davidson grunted. "Now, what do you want to know?"

"Can you just run through Willie's history. I want to make sure I get all the facts exactly right. This is going to be one *big* article. The editor promised me two whole pages ... maybe three, with photographs."

"No photographs of Willie now," Boetz put in quickly. "Not unless you want some shots of shark steaks."

"Oh!" the reporter said, and raised her fine eyebrows. "He's been ... cut up, then?"

"Yeah. We had to perform an autopsy to check on possible causes of death," Boetz smiled a ferret smile.

"I see. Can we come to that later?" Kathy Miller asked. "I wanted to go back to when Willie first arrived at your aquarium."

"I was here myself when he arrived," Boetz said.

"And you are?"

"Henry Boetz ... that's B-O-E-T-Z ... Assistant Director."

Davidson stared gloomily at the desktop and seemed happy to let his little assistant tell the story.

"It was back in August when a fisherman rolled up in his truck. He'd caught this huge fish down at the mouth of the Umgeni River. He was about two metres long and weighed a hundred and twenty kilos ... that's the *fish*, Miss Miller, not the fisherman!"

The reporter nodded. "How did he get the fish here?"

"He didn't. He kept it in the river with a rope round its tail – like a dog on a lead. Wanted to know if we were interested. He said it was some kind of shark. Now they're pretty rare round here so I set out to take a look. When I got there, the water was so low the shark looked deader than that chair you're sitting on. We threw it in the truck anyway and brought it back."

Davidson stirred and put in, "Turned out to be a bull shark. One of the meanest creatures you could ever wish to meet."

"What did you do with it?" the reporter asked.

"Put it in a tank of water to preserve it so we could have a better look later," Boetz explained. "Gave us a bit of a shock when he started stirring. In three minutes he was swimming round, as happy as Larry!"

"Larry who?"

"It's a saying, Miss Miller," Boetz said tiredly.

"Sorry. Go on."

"Well, one of the visitors gave it a name – Willie – and it sort of stuck. The crowds started flocking in to see him. Most popular creature we've ever had."

"And he recovered fully?" Kathy Miller asked.

"Not at first. For the first three weeks he wouldn't eat. We offered him all the usual kinds of fish but he wouldn't touch them. We weren't too worried. We'd seen sharks go a long time between meals."

"But he started eating in the end," the reporter nodded.

Boetz looked a little embarrassed. "A fisherman found a young manta in his nets. It was injured and he brought it to us. We reckoned with a little care we could nurse it back to fitness. We popped it in with Willie."

"That's nice!" Kathy Miller grinned. "So Willie found a friend! He'd just been lonely all that time. You're going to tell me he got his appetite back as soon as you popped that little manta ray in with him?"

Boetz shuffled his feet and arranged cigarette ends in the ashtray.

"That's right, Miss Miller. He got his appetite back," Davidson said quietly. "He ate five kilos of fish meat in one swallow."

"Wow!" the reporter said, scribbling quickly.

"Yeah," the Assistant Director added. "He ate that manta ray in one swallow."

Kathy Miller looked up slowly. "That's horrible," she said, and swallowed hard.

Davidson shrugged. "Sharks are attracted by the signals sick fish give off, did you know that? That's why sharks are so important in the seas. They clean up the sick and the dead – a bit like vultures. Seems all Willie wanted was a bit of real live sport to start eating properly again."

The reporter smiled a tight smile. "I don't think our readers would want to know that. Anyway, Willie started eating after that ... accident?"

"Hmm," Boetz said, and spread his hands. "We threw him ray meat and even shark meat. It just seems he preferred to take care of himself. Any time we put something live in the tank he ate it. We put some of the rarest fish we've ever had in that tank because we were short of space. Willie ate them all. Some dusky sharks survived for a while – even a female dogfish, until he got hungry and sliced her in two."

"This must have cost you a lot of money," the reporter said.

"Yes," Davidson said. "Of course he was still bringing in the visitors, so he was paying his way."

"Slight problem with tank maintenance, though," Boetz put in. Davidson gave him a slow glare, and the little man felt he'd said just a little too much.

"Tank maintenance, Mr Boetz?" the reporter asked, and raised her pencil.

"Yeah. We got to keep the tanks clean. Otherwise the water turns bad, goes cloudy, starts to smell. You can't put chlorine in like you would at a swimming pool – you'd kill the fish. You have to send divers in to scrape the bottom and the sides of the tank."

"I see. Why was that a problem?"

The two men looked around the room. They seemed to be interested in anything and everything but the reporter and her notebook. Suddenly Kathy Miller's eyes widened. "Oh, I see! Willie started attacking the divers!"

"No!" Davidson said quickly. "Don't print that! He ... er ... just started showing a sort of interest in them. In fact, the men refused to go into the tank with him."

"Willie was becoming a problem, then," the reporter said, scenting a new and interesting story.

"No!" Davidson said sharply. "He was a real pet, was old

Willie. If we'd had a problem we could always have set him free into the sea again."

Kathy Miller thought about this for a few moments. "No, you couldn't. You can't set a shark free once it's lost its fear of humans. Why, you'd get the blame for every shark attack off this coast for the next ten years!"

Davidson looked uncomfortable. "Doesn't matter. Willie died before it became a problem."

"Wasn't that lucky for you!" the reporter said. "What did he die of?"

"We found him dead when we came down at dawn today," Boetz said.

"But you cut him up – you said so. You're marine-life specialists. You must have some idea of why he died. I have to be able to tell my readers *something*. Otherwise they may think you had something to do with his death."

Davidson took out a large handkerchief and mopped at his neck, which was turning hot and red. "We found his liver was discoloured in one lobe. We reckon he died of liver failure.

Kathy Miller scribbled that down and closed her notebook. "Sad case, Mr Davidson. But I think it could well make the front page. The local people will be very upset."

"We cried buckets when we found him," Boetz nodded.

"Thank you for your help," the reporter said. She smiled brightly and left.

Davidson rocked back in his chair until it creaked. The newspaper lay on the desk. The front-page headline read in huge letters, *Willie Dies Suddenly From Liver Failure*. Boetz's skinny body looked as limp as a dead fish.

The Director lit another cigarette and his hand was shaking as he put it to his lips. "Reckon we got away with it?"

"It was only a *shark*, for goodness' sake!" Boetz groaned.

"Not to those people out there," Dave Davidson said. "And not to you and me. You know that what we did was nothing short of murder."

"His time was up," Boetz sighed. "Everyone and everything has a time to die. This was Willie's time. "The little man leaned forward. "Would you rather be talking to Miss Miller about a dead diver? No."

Davidson sniffed. "I just wish we hadn't had to tell so many lies. I feel really bad about that. I want to tell the truth. Set the record straight."

"Not now. Not unless you want to be torn apart by all Willie's human friends out there. Don't worry, the time will come when we can tell the truth."

"In the meantime we're getting away with murder?"

Boetz nodded and tilted the felt hat to the back of his head. He seemed quite pleased at the idea. Blue cigarette smoke floated in the weak, yellow light. The scent of the smoke couldn't kill the smell of dead fish. Davidson looked sick, but Boetz felt like one of the gangsters in the films he enjoyed. "Give it time, Dave. Give it time. There's a time for everything."

Some years later, the Director of Durban Aquarium "confessed" to the murder of Willie. Just as Boetz predicted, the public had forgotten about Willie by then.

But at the time of Willie's death, the truth was hidden from the public. That bull shark must have been one of the few sharks who was ever really loved by the public.Willie probably deserves a place in the record books as the world's most popular shark.

Popularity is hard to measure, of course. Other features of sharks are easier to measure. Some of the most impressive facts are...

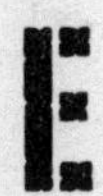

Shark Records

1. Largest

The largest shark, the whale shark, usually grows to 15 metres in length and is the largest living fish. One caught in 1919 measured 17.98 metres and weighed nearly 43 tonnes. But it is harmless to humans – it feeds on plankton (microscopic sea organisms).

2. Smallest

The spined pygmy shark is just 150 millimetres in length.

3. Oldest

Today's sharks are almost identical to some that lived 160 million years ago. This makes them one of the oldest unchanged creatures on Earth. Human beings developed from apes only two to four million years ago.

FACT FILE

4. Hardest bite

There is a machine for measuring the power of a shark's bite. It is called a gnathodynamometer. It shows that a small dusky shark, just 2 metres long, can give 22 tonnes of pressure at the tips of its teeth. A great white shark can cut a 300-kilo fish in half with just one bite.

5. Fastest

Some great white sharks can reach speeds of 64 kilometres per hour. This makes them one of the fastest fish ... and the hardest to escape from.

6. Thickest skin

Whale sharks have skin 100 millimetres thick – the thickest of any creature. Harpoons have been seen to bounce off it.

7. Biggest eggs

Whale sharks also lay the biggest eggs of any living creature. They are 300 millimetres long, and rectangular. Their young are 350 millimetres long when they hatch, yet they grow to a length of 13 metres – almost 40 times as large.

8. First in England

John Hawkins was an English slave trader. He brought the first shark to England in 1569, during the reign of Elizabeth I.

9. Furthest

Scientists can follow sharks using electronic "tags", which give off radio signals. The greatest distance travelled by a "tagged" shark was 1,850 kilometres – between New York and the Cape Verde islands off the western coast of Africa.

F A C T F I L E

10. Rarest

Some types of sharks are so rare they have hardly ever been seen by humans. The rarest is probably one discovered in 1976. It lives deep in the ocean during the day, and never comes closer than 30 metres from the surface at night. This 5-metre shark was named "megamouth" by the scientists who discovered it, because of its large mouth. Since that first sighting in 1976, a shark of this type has only been seen five more times. They have all been males, so perhaps the rarest shark is the female megamouth, which has never been seen! Of course, there are probably some shark types still to be discovered.

RED DEATH

If sharks terrify people, then the height of bravery must be to struggle against a shark in their own domain – water. It takes a special kind of person to overcome their fear. A person like Shirley O'Neill...

California, USA, November 1963

Mrs O'Neill picked up the newspaper from the front porch and carried it into the house. Her daughter sat on the couch in front of the television and watched the news report from Dallas. Her face was a mask of pain, her eyes close to tears.

The announcer spoke in a low voice. "Police believe that shots came from a book store. Surgeons operated to remove the bullets, but President Kennedy died within an hour of the shooting."

Mrs O'Neill placed the newspaper on the couch beside her daughter. "There's a picture on the front page, Shirley," she said.

The young woman picked up her paper. *President Kennedy Dead*, the headline said. But it was the picture that caught Shirley's eye and held her. "Oh, the poor woman! " she moaned.

Mrs O'Neill looked over her daughter's shoulder. The picture showed the President's wife in the back seat of the open-topped car. She held her husband's head in her lap. Blood stained her suit.

"She wasn't hurt," Mrs O'Neill said gently.

"No," Shirley said. "Neither was I with Albert. But you have to live with the memory. I know exactly how she must have felt."

"I know, I know," Mrs O'Neill said. "I was hoping you'd got over it."

Shirley shook her head, rose to her feet and switched the television off. "You never get over something as horrible as that."

"I suppose not," her mother said helplessly. "I suppose not."

Four years ago her daughter had left home to go swimming with her boyfriend, Albert Kogler. When she left home that morning she'd been in a good mood.It was the last time Mrs O'Neill could remember her daughter laughing.

Albert had been a really nice young man. Mrs O'Neill approved of him. He was a little shy – a little awkward with women. But Shirley had enough bounce and energy for both of them. She'd been going out with him since they'd graduated from high school together. Mrs O'Neill would have been happy if they'd said they wanted to get married – but they were taking their time about that.

They argued from time to time, but they seemed to enjoy the arguments. Albert liked Frank Sinatra, while Shirley preferred some wild young singer called Elvis Presley. Mrs O'Neill let them squabble over the record player and smiled quietly to herself. Shirley was happy.

Until that day – 7 May 1959. Shirley left the house. Laughing. "Going swimming with Albert," she called to her mother.

"Whereabouts?"

"Baker's Beach."

"Take care."

"I will."

When it got to eight that evening Mrs O'Neill was beginning to wonder where Shirley had got to. It wasn't like her to go to Albert's for supper without telephoning. Shirley's mother was just about to call Albert's house, when the doorbell jangled.

Mrs O'Neill saw the policeman first. Then the small figure huddled beside him, shivering in a white hospital robe. It was her daughter.

"Mrs O'Neill?"

"What's happened?"

"Can we come in?"

The woman put an arm round her daughter's shoulder and led her to the couch. The girl was stiff and cold, and her pale eyes were blank. She stared into the flickering fire and her lips moved silently.

The policeman stood awkwardly and watched. "What happened? Is she all right?" Mrs O'Neill repeated.

"She's all right, ma'am," the policeman said slowly. "But her friend, Mr Albert Kogler, died late this afternoon down in Baker's Bay."

"Drowned?" Mrs O'Neill cried.

"No," Shirley said. "No, not drowned." She continued to stare into the fire, but began talking quickly, as much to herself as to her mother. "We were sunbathing on the beach. Like we always do. Like we've done a hundred times before. But it was hot. We just went in the water to cool off."

Her mother nodded to the policeman to sit in the fireside chair while she wrapped an arm around her daughter's shoulders. Shirley went on, "We'd been in the water for about fifteen minutes and were only about forty metres out when he said, 'We're pretty far out now. Let's not go any farther, it'd be too dangerous.' We were treading water as we were talking. We were just about to start back and I was looking away from him towards the Golden Gate. That's when I heard him scream."

Mrs O'Neill felt the girl shudder. "What was it?"

"I turned around and saw this big thing flap up into the air. I didn't know whether it was a fin or a tail. I knew it was some kind of fish. There was a thrashing in the water and I knew he was struggling with it. It must have been pretty big. Then Albert shouted, 'It's a shark ... get out of here!'"

"There's never been a shark this far north," the policeman said. He seemed to be trying to apologize.

"I started swimming back," the girl continued. "I swam a few strokes – breaststroke, but very fast – and then I thought to myself, 'I can't just leave him here.' I was scared, and I didn't know what to do, but I knew I couldn't leave him."

"What else could you do?" her mother asked.

"I turned around and swam a couple of strokes back. He kept screaming. It was a horrible scream. It was as if the fish was eating him alive. All I could see was blood all over the water. He was shouting. 'Help me! Help me!' I grabbed for his arm but it was ... it was almost bitten through. I had to put my arm around him to drag him back."

She stopped and stared at the flames, as if they held the picture of that dreadful moment.

The policeman took up the story. "I was on the top of the cliff. I knew I'd never get down there in time to help. All I could do was radio from the car."

Now Mrs O'Neill understood his guilt. He'd had to watch, helpless, while her daughter wrestled Albert from the grip of a shark. She smiled at the officer to show that she understood.

The policeman took a deep breath and said, "I've never seen so much courage – not on the streets of San Francisco – not even in the war. Your daughter deserves a medal, Mrs O'Neill. The water was churning with the shark. It was wild. The water was red around Albert and he seemed to be waving and yelling at someone to get back to shore. That's when I saw Shirley. She was swimming *towards* him. She was ignoring all his warnings. It must have taken her twenty minutes to get him that last forty metres. A fisherman threw her a line and hauled her up the last part. Where did she get the strength from?" he shook his head again.

"I stayed with him until the ambulance took him to hospital," the girl said. "I prayed for him, Mom. I said every prayer I knew. I did. I tried."

"That must have been a comfort to him," Mrs O'Neill said.

Shirley nodded. The shock was thawing now and her eyes were beginning to fill with tears. "He died, Mom. He died in hospital. I didn't save him."

"You couldn't have done more," the policeman said, and his voice was almost angry. "For God's sake. You couldn't have done more. No one could."

"I went in the ambulance with him. I held his hand. I talked to him. I think he knew I was there."

"Shush, shush," her mother said, and wiped her daughter's tears with a handkerchief. "The doctor will give you something to help you sleep."

The girl pulled away and looked at her mother for the first time since she had come home. Her eyes were full of horror. "Oh, no. I never want to sleep! You see, I know what I'll dream about."

And for some months the nightmares haunted her every time she closed her eyes. Mrs O'Neill knew that the thing that pulled Shirley out of this deadly cycle of the nightmares was the letter that arrived from the President's office in early 1960.

The girl opened it and stared. "Well?" her mother asked.

"It's from President Kennedy – well, from his secretary, anyway," she said, and for the first time in months she managed a small smile. It was a smile of wonder. "He says the President wants to award me the Young American People's Medal of Valor.

I have go to the White House to receive it."

Her mother nodded. "That night when ... it happened ... that night the policeman, Sergeant Day, said you should get something."

The girl was bewildered, but it was what she needed. Something to look forward to. Something that acknowledged what she'd been through.

"He was so kind to me. Knew all about Albert ... all about the shark," Shirley said, as she and her mother flew home after the presentation. "He's a great man – a great President."

And three years later she was looking at the picture on the front of the paper. "I know how she felt, Mom. Just holding him. Waiting for the ambulance. Watching his life blood flowing away ... and praying."

Mrs O'Neill took the paper from her daughter. She had her own prayer. A prayer that the nightmares wouldn't return. "It's not only the victims who suffer, is it?" she sighed.

FACT FILE

If a Shark Attacks

There is generally no reason to fear shark attacks if you are sensible. The following rules will make sure you are unlikely to be one of the 100 people around the world who are attacked every year. Some advice is obvious, some common sense, and some very difficult to follow if you suddenly come face to face with a great white shark. It is easy to say "Don't panic!" – but probably much harder to do!

1. Don't swim in areas where sharks have been sighted.

2. Don't swim at night – that's the time when sharks prefer to feed.

3. If you spot a shark, get out of the water as quickly and quietly as you can. Splashes and loud noises attract sharks – so swim smoothly.

4. Don't swim alone in risky waters. Have someone as a lookout.

5. Don't wear contrasting colours – for example black and white. Sharks can't see colours, but they can see sharp contrasts.

6. Don't wear jewellery – flashing metal attracts sharks.

7. If you can't get out of the water, then keep the shark in view – sharks rarely attack humans who are facing them.

8. Leave the water if you have even the slightest cut – sharks' powerful ability to scent blood will attract them from a kilometre away.

9. If you've been fishing then remember that the blood of the fish you catch could also attract a shark.

10. If everything else fails, then scream at the shark (it sometimes scares them off) or punch it on the snout.

Shark defences

Over the centuries many people have tried to come up with a defence against sharks. Some have been more successful than others…

1. Stripy suits

Sharks are supposed to be afraid of banded sea snakes. So, dress a swimmer in a wetsuit that has black and white hoops around it and the shark will swim off in terror. Does it work? As sharks are attracted to contrasting colours, it's not surprising that an experienced diver said it had absolutely no effect at all. 0/10

2. Shark armour

Metal suits made of a sort of chain-mail will stop small sharks from tearing lumps of flesh from a swimmer. It has worked in tests with 2-metre sharks. However a large shark would still almost certainly do some serious damage with the sheer power of its jaws. Anyway, it could carry off the diver (and the suit) in one piece. 5/10

3. Shark nets

Placing a net across part of a bay makes it safer for swimmers. The success can be seen in the number of sharks caught each year. They have been tried in Sydney (1937) with fair success. But on one South African beach the shark attacks *increased* after nets were tried! 5/10

4. Spear guns

By themselves spear guns don't work too well. The shark has to be struck in the brain and that's a very small target. Sharks can be stabbed many times in the body and still keep attacking. 1/10

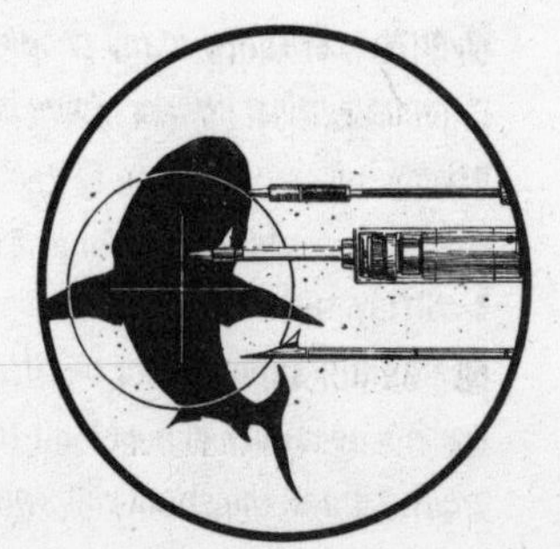

5. Powerheads

Attach an explosive charge to a spear gun and you have a much more useful weapon. They still require the diver to be an accurate shot, however. 6/10

6. Gas injection darts

These are another device attached to a spear gun. The dart sticks into the shark and fills it with carbon dioxide gas, so that it blows up like a balloon. When it floats to the surface it quickly suffocates. But to do this, the diver has to hit the body from the side or from below. Head-on shots don't work – and if a shark is attacking, it will come at you head on. 4/10

7. Electric shark repellents

Built into a wetsuit, electric shark repellents will give the shark a shock if it so much as touches a diver. They work, but they're so expensive they have not been used very much. 7/10

8. Shark screen

A sort of life belt with a bag hanging under it. Once the swimmer is in the bag s/he becomes invisible to a shark. Very useful for crashed aeroplane passengers or sunken boat survivors. Obviously no use to a sport/fun swimmer. 8/10

9. Shark chasers

Chemicals that a shark scents, dislikes and swims away from. Various types have been tested. All claim to make a swimmer completely safe. In fact, none of them work. 0/10

10. Bubble barrier

The theory was that bubbles from divers' gas bottles drove off sharks. There were many experiments with barriers of bubbles.

FACT

FILE

The plan was that humans could swim behind a bubble curtain, while sharks would be turned away. Great idea. Unfortunately they don't seem to work. 0/10

THE LIARS

Sometimes it's difficult to uncover the truth about shark attacks. The facts are hidden from the public because they are too horrible. The people with the facts tell lies. That's what happened in the case of HMS *Birkenhead...*

The Admiralty Offices, London, England, April 1852

A shaft of sunlight fell from the high window of the office and struck the desk. Dust floated down on to sheets of writing paper, quill pens and a pot of ink.

After what seemed like an age, the man in the naval uniform moved and the dust whirled up and sparkled in the light. "No," he said. "It's a remarkable story. The witnesses are honest people. We must publish the stories ... but we will cut out any mention of sharks. The men who died were heroes. We want the families to remember them going peacefully to their rest. We don't want to leave them with memories of the men being torn to shreds by these monster fish, do we?"

"No, sir," the young officer said. He had been standing to attention in front of the Admiral's desk for ten minutes, while the old man thought about the problem. Now the Admiral invited him to sit down.

"So let's get clear what we're going to say. Take me through it from the beginning, Lieutenant Oliver."

"Yes, sir. The frigate *Birkenhead* of the Royal Navy was sailing around the Cape of Good Hope with a crew of one hundred and thirty-four men, under the command of Captain Robert Salmond. Their passengers included four hundred and ninety English soldiers, under the command of Colonel Seton. There were twenty-five wives and thirty-one children with the soldiers. Six hundred and eighty people in total."

"Put in the time and date," the Admiral ordered.

"Yes, sir. At 2.00 a.m. on the morning of 26 February this year, the ship struck a reef just one mile off the coast of Africa at a place called Danger Point."

"Hah! Well named." The Admiral sighed. "We won't put any blame on Captain Salmond for hitting the reef. Don't want to destroy that chap's reputation, do we?"

"No, sir. We could claim *Birkenhead* had a damaged rudder. Currents forced her on to the reef. Act of God."

"Good. I like that. Act of God. Make a note of that, Lieutenant."

"Yes, sir."

"Carry on."

"Water flooded into the bows of the ship and some drowned immediately. Everyone rushed on to the deck. Colonel Seton told the soldiers they were under the command of the ship's captain. They must do everything he ordered. The Captain then ordered that the women and children be placed in a rowing boat, and another sergeant was sent to separate the wives and husbands – by force, if necessary."

"Imagine that, Lieutenant. Those women going to safety knowing they were leaving their husbands to drown. Cruel, Lieutenant, cruel." He went silent again for a minute.

The Lieutenant cleared his throat. "Shall I carry on, sir?"

"Yes, yes."

"The second life-boat was launched with room for just thirty people. There were still six hundred men on deck when the last boat left. That's when there is some confusion among the reports. As the ship dipped into the water many men were thrown in. It was dark, of course, but the survivors could hear sounds in the night. Screams. Thrashing in the water. That's when the first sharks began to attack. A mast had crashed on the deck and killed some of the men. It was probably the blood from that accident that attracted the sharks, as much as anything."

"We'll leave that part out, if you don't mind, Lieutenant. Get on to that part about the courage of the survivors.

"There must have been about two hundred men left on deck – soldiers and sailors – when Captain Salmond climbed a little way up the foremast. He called for the men's attention. Everything went quiet as the Captain spoke to them."

"You have a note of his exact words?"

"Yes. There were enough people in the boats nearby to hear. They all agree," the Lieutenant said.

The Admiral nodded. "Go on. Read me Captain Salmond's last words."

"He said, 'It is every man for himself now. Your only chance, if you can swim, is to jump into the water and try to cling to anything floating. But I beg of you, avoid the rowing boat with the women and children. It is already overloaded. I am asking you, in fact, to stay where you are.'"

The Admiral repeated the last words slowly. "'I am asking you to stay where you are'. He was asking them to die so that the women and children might live. I am asking you, he said. Not ordering. Asking. How many men decided to try to save themselves, Lieutenant?"

"Just three, sir."

"Three. Out of two hundred. Read me the report of the officer who survived," the Admiral ordered.

The Lieutenant sifted through the sheets of parchment, then read from one. "Every man did what he had been asked to do. There was not a shout nor a murmur among them until the ship finally went down. The officers had heard their captain's request and followed his words as if he'd asked them to board ship, not sink to the bottom of the sea. There was only one difference. I have never seen men board ship with the lack of fuss or confusion that I saw in those brave men who went to their deaths."

Again the old man nodded in admiration. "You have that report from Lieutenant Girardot?"

"Yes, sir."

"Let me check it. I think that is one we don't want published."

The Lieutenant handed over another sheet and the Admiral read it. "'I remained on deck until the boat sank. I was dragged under water by the suction of the sinking ship. A man caught my leg. I freed myself by kicking him and got to the surface. I hung on to some pieces of wood and remained in the water for five hours. Practically all those who found themselves in the water without clothes were taken by sharks. Hundreds of sharks surrounded us, and I saw a number of men seized right next to me, but as I was dressed the sharks preferred the others.'"

"Gruesome, sir."

"Yes, Lieutenant. If the ship had sunk in the daytime, then most of the men would have been dressed. It seems that sharks go for bare flesh, but not so much for the clothed ones. Bad luck, that. Have a word with Lieutenant Girardot and tell him to keep quiet about the sharks. I suppose he managed to swim the mile to shore. How many others made it?"

"Just sixty, sir."

"Colonel Seton?"

"Couldn't swim, sir."

"Captain Salmond?"

"Thrown into the sea shortly after he made his speech to the men. Struck by one of the falling masts."

"And you say the total death toll was four hundred and fifty-five lives?"

"Yes, sir."

"Release the story to the newspapers. But just the story we have agreed. Let the world see how bravely British sailors and soldiers can die. And how unselfishly. 'I am asking you to stay where you are.' What a line! A line to be remembered whenever our men fight."

The Lieutenant rose to his feet, saluted, and turned towards the door.

"Lieutenant!" the Admiral called. The young man was reaching for the brass door-handle.

"Sir?"

"No sharks, remember. Too horrible. No sharks."

"No sharks, sir." And he left the room, closing the door quietly behind him.

The sunlight slanted through the high windows and fell on the paper in front of the old man. He looked at the report again, slowly crumpled it in his fist and dropped it into a basket at the side of his chair.

The dust settled on the desk, so it looked as if that report had never been written.

The truth came out in private letters written by survivors, like Lieutenant Girardot, who wrote to their families. The Navy never admitted the claims about shark attacks.

FACT FILE

Shark Bites: Ten Tales

All shark attacks are horrific. But some reports have been even stranger than fiction…

1. Queensland, Australia, 1951. A fine yacht was found floating on the Fitzroy River with not a single living soul aboard. Another *Marie Celeste* perhaps? No – for there was a single *dead* person aboard. He was identified as Dr Joske from Adelaide … and he had died of the most terrible injuries. His stomach had been torn open and one of his legs was missing. A murder mystery? Or perhaps a shark attack…? There have, after all, been recorded cases of sharks leaping on to boats as they follow fish being reeled in from the deck.

2. Tuamotu Islands, South Pacific, 1900. A pearl diver was working underwater when a shark appeared. Still underwater, the man hid in a coral cave, but the shark appeared suddenly behind him. As it attacked, the expert swimmer threw himself on to the back of the shark and thrust his hands into its gills. This drove the shark wild with panic. It rushed into shallow water where it swam madly around in a pool, unable to find a passage back to the sea. The man was then able to climb on to a rock. He examined his cuts and grazes and became furious. He paddled back to the stranded shark and punched it as hard as he could on the snout. The startled shark thrashed its way back to deeper water and fled!

3. Broome, Australia, 1949. Mary Passaris was enjoying a swim off the Australian coast when she was attacked by a shark. It tore the poor girl's forearm off, but she bravely managed to escape, and made it to the safety of the beach. As she recovered in hospital, she received an unexpected present. The 3-metre shark had been caught and cut open. Inside its stomach was Mary's hand … complete with a treasured gold ring. The ring was taken from the finger and given back to the girl. She was able to wear it again … but on the other hand, of course.

4. Torres Strait, New Guinea, 1937. One of the most gruesome attacks was on a pearl fisherman, Iona Asai. He was swimming along the bottom of the sea, collecting pearl oysters, when he suddenly came face to face with a shark. The shark seemed as surprised as the fisherman and grabbed the first thing it could … his head! Iona struggled with his head in the shark's mouth and managed to poke the creature in the eyes. The shark released him and he swam to the surface. Despite horrific injuries to his neck, the fisherman survived. In the same spot, 20 years before, a pearl fisherman had dived off his boat, head first into the jaws of a shark … amazingly, he too survived.

5. Tuscany, Italy, 1989. A distressed Gian Costanzo told police of the horrifying death of his father, Luciano, as they had dived off the Italian coast. A six-metre shark had attacked him and swallowed him, Gian reported. The local people were worried. That sort of story would scare away the tourists who brought prosperity to the region. So a shark hunt was launched, but nothing was found … except a lead diving belt, air tanks, and a pair of flippers. Had the shark undressed

Luciano before swallowing him? Or was the report an invention? Was Luciano in fact alive and well, and sharing the huge insurance money his son would collect? Sharks are rare in these waters, but they can make convenient scapegoats. Truth or fiction? Nothing was ever proved.

6. Miami, Florida, USA, 1985. Not everyone is successful in faking a shark attack. Sometimes the police know more about sharks than the people carrying out the fraud. A boy was suspected of stealing his girlfriend's car, money and jewellery. But before he could be arrested, he died tragically in the jaws of a shark. His friend described how they'd been out fishing together, when the suspect had decided to go swimming. A black fin had appeared and the boy had vanished in a swirl of red. But the experienced policeman the boy told knew better. He said, "Sharks cruise with their fins above the water – but when they attack, they attack from below. You're lying!" He was right. The "dead" boy was found two weeks later in Los Angeles. As the Pacific fishermen will tell you, "It is only the one you do not see that kills."

7. Jamaica, 1993. Chris and Stuart Newman of Middlesbrough, England, attempted to become the first to paddle a canoe from Europe to America. They arrived in Jamaica, exhausted and starving, and with a gruelling tale of shark attacks.

They had run out of food, and caught a dolphin which they cut up and ate. The blood of the dolphin attracted white-tip sharks. The canoe was capsized and damaged by the sharks, which circled round them for four hours. They were able to right the canoe when the sharks disappeared the next day.

As Chris and Stuart staggered ashore in Jamaica, they came

across another type of "shark" – while a local fisherman offered them some of his catch to eat, other locals tried to steal the equipment from the damaged canoe!

8. Japan, 1992. One of the most modest shark-fighters was Yoshiaki Ueda, a 71-year-old Japanese fisherman who went out fishing for horse mackerel. He single-handedly fought off an attack by a three-metre shark ... then had a bigger problem fighting off the television and newspaper reporters who wanted to hear his story. "There was an attack and I hit the shark on the nose with an oar. I beat it. That's it. Now leave me alone, because I want to get back to my fishing!" The reporters told his story anyway – but the shark grew to four metres, then five metres in the reports!

9. Unconfirmed place and date. One story is repeated in many shark books – but the books forget to say one thing. The man who first reported it said, "My readers have already heard that sharks will swallow any kind of garbage, but I'm afraid the following will be too much even for their belief." He then repeats the old story that a shark was cut open and a man was found inside. He was complete except for his head. The shark had not digested the man's body because it was wearing a suit of armour!

Can *you* swallow that sort of garbage?

10. Melbourne, Australia, 1964. To be attacked by a shark and lose a leg, you have to be extremely unlucky. But to be attacked *twice* by a shark and lose a leg sounds like incredible bad fortune. To lose the *same* leg twice to a shark is surely impossible! It happened to Henry Bource. While swimming off the Australian coast in 1964, he was attacked by a shark and lost the lower part of his right leg. Four years later, he went back to do some filming. He was attacked again – and the shark made off with his artificial leg!

THE LOG OF THE SS ANTONIO

Sharks have been blamed for taking many human lives. Just occasionally, though, there is a really unusual story about a shark that saved a life...

Somewhere in the South Atlantic, 19 June 1971

Miguel thinks we're going to die.

He wants me to write this report before we do. It seems important to him. He wants his wife and daughter to know what happened.

"Why don't you write it yourself?" I asked him.

He looked at me as if I was stupid. "I can't write," he shrugged.

Miguel isn't much good at anything. Of all the people to share my last days with, why did it have to be him, God? He's Miguel Vargas, a whingeing, boot-licking little deckhand on the good ship SS Antonio, out of Southampton, bound for New Zealand.

And me? I'm Carlo Pellini, senior deckhand on the same ship. Except we aren't on the ship, because it's somewhere at the bottom of the South Atlantic. I am presently senior deckhand on a rubber dinghy. Don't ask me for my position. I'm not a navigator, just a labourer. We're somewhere south of the Equator,

I know that. I just wish we were further south, because it would be cooler there.

Miguel wants me to tell you about the sinking. He thinks someone should know what happened. He thinks the owners should pay a lot of money to his wife when they finally find us dead. He says it was the owners' fault.

Fair enough, Miguel, you could have a point. Me? I've nobody to claim money for me on my death. No one to care. That's why I sailed on a floating rust-bucket like the Antonio. I don't care.

Before we left England, the chief engineer was complaining about the boilers. "She'll not get out of harbour," he told the captain.

The skipper had a look, and called someone in to patch the boiler. That made us a day late, of course. We'd lose money on the contract if we delivered late. So we had to go faster. And faster meant more strain on the boilers, didn't it?

We didn't sail on Thursday as we were due. We sailed on Friday.

One day, Miguel came to my cabin like a headless chicken. He'd heard the skipper arguing with the engineer. "The boilers are going to blow up!" Miguel whined. "We will all end up at the bottom of the sea!"

"I've sailed in worse ships than this," I told him. "And I'm still here to tell the tale."

That cheered him up. "You are a lucky sailor, Carlo," he said. "I'll stick with you."

He did. Like glue. That's how we were together on the stern when the ship blew last night.

The deck trembled under our feet and the ship shuddered. A second later, the explosion lifted the bridge into the air and split the hull in two. Miguel and I were sheltered by a hatch cover. That hatch cover took the worst of the blast and the scalding steam and oil.

I knew that no one below decks and no one on the bridge could have survived. I also knew that we'd be shark bait ourselves in less than five minutes.

After the explosion, there was a long silence – or maybe I was just deafened. I stood on my shaking legs and looked down the deck. It was already beginning to tilt towards the foaming sea. Miguel was on his knees, praying.

I grabbed his collar and dragged him to his feet. "Life raft!" I yelled. He looked at me stupidly. There was a small rubber dinghy strapped to the afterdeck. I started to unfasten one side, and saw him slowly start on the other side. He seemed to have given up on life already. His lips were still moving in some kind of prayer. But he did it.

The ship was sliding steadily below the water. We wouldn't need to launch the dinghy. Just sit there and let the water reach us.

I slid down the deck towards one of the large lifeboats. It was splintered and useless, but I tore at the canvas cover and grabbed a survival pack. Water, food, a first-aid kit and a flare pistol. Then I tried to get back to the rubber dinghy. The deck was sloping steeply now. It was like trying to climb a frozen waterfall.

Miguel stretched out a paddle. I grabbed it and he hauled me aboard, just as the water began slapping at my boots. He managed a faint smile. "Start paddling!" I shouted, as the dinghy slid into the steaming foam. He didn't move. "Paddle!" I screamed, grabbing the other one and clawing at the water. "The ship will suck us under as it goes down!" I panted. "We have to get as far away as possible."

He finally understood. Fear made him paddle twice as fast as me.

Somehow we made it. The SS Antonio dived into her grave more gracefully than she'd ever sailed above it.

Miguel was praying again. Maybe his God was looking down on us after all.

But it's growing dark now. Night comes suddenly when you're near the Equator.

If we're alive tomorrow I'll write more.

If not, then goodbye, whoever you are.

20 June 1971

It was cold last night. We were thirsty. When I dropped off to sleep I almost rolled over into the sea.

Miguel dragged me back. I was lucky. Lucky Carlo.

Really, it's a matter of my luck against Miguel's. He has so many superstitions. "We sailed on a Friday," he wailed. "Bad luck!"

But I have the feather of a wren in my pocket. Carried it for twenty years. It's still there. That's protecting me.

So Miguel and I argue about "luck". It's a waste of time and precious energy. "Look at it sensibly," I tell him. "We're on a shipping lane. A hundred ships a day pass somewhere near here."

"Or a mile away," he says gloomily.

"We have a distress rocket," I say, showing him the gun from the survival pack.

"Only one shell," he whinges. "Only one chance."

"We have enough water for three days..."

"But it's so hot here," he sighs.

"We could be worse off," I tell him. "Someone will miss *Antonio*. Three days for them to find us."

Then he turns those big, brown, mournful eyes on the horizon. "If the sharks don't get us first..." he whispers.

I don't have an answer to that.

He said he saw the first shark last night. I told him he'd just seen the shadow of a wave.

But at first light I saw the black fin for myself. I thought it might just be passing by. It was still there an hour later. Swimming in a large circle.

How does it *know*? Miguel groans and starts that whimpering and praying.

"It can't get us while we're in the dinghy," I say.

"When we die, it will eat us," he says quietly.

"If you're dead, you won't care," I tell him viciously.

He's right, though. Just the thought makes me shiver. If I'm going to die, I want to sink to the bottom of the sea and rest in the sand. The thought of what that shark would do is too horrible to bear.

Miguel is weak. He'll die before me. If I throw him over the side maybe that'll satisfy the shark. Maybe it'll leave me to die in peace.

I'm not afraid of dying.

It's just that black fin...

21 June 1971

Two black fins.

Maybe more.

Two days and no ships. Smudges of smoke on the horizon. I daren't risk the flare.

There's not enough water for this heat. My lips are cracking. Miguel is so still he could be dead.

He asked me to tell his Maria how much he loves her. So, there you go, Maria. Whoever you are, whatever you are, he loves you.

He loved you.

I'll see that the sharks don't get him. I'll wrap him tight in the canvas cover from the dinghy, weight it down, and throw him over when his time comes.

They won't get him.

They're getting bolder now. Their circles are smaller. I'll swear they're getting impatient.

Not long now, my beauties. I'm almost tempted to dangle a hand in the water. Then, when you come to take a nibble, blast you with the only shell in the distress rocket. If I'm going to die I want to take one of you with me.

I hate you. Why should you live and not me? Or even Miguel?

He woke up a moment ago. He smiled at me. He went back to sleep. He's weak.

So am I. Time to go. I want to slip away peacefully like an old cat lying in the sun.

I've said goodbye to Miguel. Covered him in the canvas to keep the sun off him. Now it's goodbye to you, stranger.

Hope you have better luck than me.

22 June 1971

Maybe it was my lucky wren's feather. Maybe it was Miguel's prayers. But somebody's God was looking down on us. We are alive. We are aboard the steamship Calcutta Pride and Miguel is pestering me to write a letter to his Maria.

Later, Miguel, later. We have lots of time. We have the rest of our lives thanks to some sort of miracle ... and the greed of those sharks.

I lay for a long time after I'd written the last entry in this log. I was waiting for sleep. And I knew that when I fell asleep, I'd never wake up. At last I'd stopped caring.

All I wanted was to be dead when those sharks finally took me.

The sharks were getting angrier. My eyes were closed but I could hear the swishing of their fins in the water. The waves their fins made slapped against the side of the dinghy.

At last I fell asleep. So deep I don't think I even dreamed.

I must have slept for an hour, because, when I woke, the sun was lower in the sky.

But it was the sharp thump on the side of the raft that woke me. The dinghy tilted and jarred me awake. Something was hitting us. Every twenty seconds that thump again.

I lifted my head to look over the side. A shark rushed towards the raft and swam below, catching it and tilting it with that powerful fin. "Dinner time, is it?" I croaked. I reached for the oar to beat it away. I hadn't the strength.

I managed to sit up. I watched that fin circle and return for another attack. Then I froze. For, just at that moment the dinghy rode higher on the swell of the sea and I saw the ship. A small tramp steamer. It was close but sailing away from us. We were so low in the water it had failed to see us.

I fumbled for the flare pistol. My aching hands tightened round the butt. I raised it in the air ... fumbled and dropped it. It hit the rubber side of the raft and bounced. I watched in helpless agony as it rose in the air. That's when luck played its part. The raft tilted slightly, just a shade – and the pistol fell back inside, and not into the waiting sea.

This time I gripped it firmly, wrapped a finger round the trigger and pulled. Nothing. The pistol was jammed. I was going to die, watching that little ship sail over the horizon.

I was ready to throw the gun at that shark. It knew how close we were to being saved. It wanted to tip the dinghy before we could be rescued. Then I remembered the safety catch on the pistol.

For some reason my eyes filled with tears when I realized my own stupidity. I slipped the catch off, raised the pistol in the air and pulled the trigger.

The rocket exploded with a thrust that almost sent me backwards into the hungry sea. But somehow I clung on.

The red flare blossomed like a beautiful rose in the darkening, purple sky. I closed my eyes. If they hadn't seen it then I was dead again.

Hope is a cruel thing. I crushed that hope inside me. I waited to die.

I think I fell asleep again.

They woke me when they lifted me out of the raft.

"You're all right, mate," someone said.

"Miguel?" was all I could say.

"He'll be fine," the voice said and laid me in a bunk on the little ship.

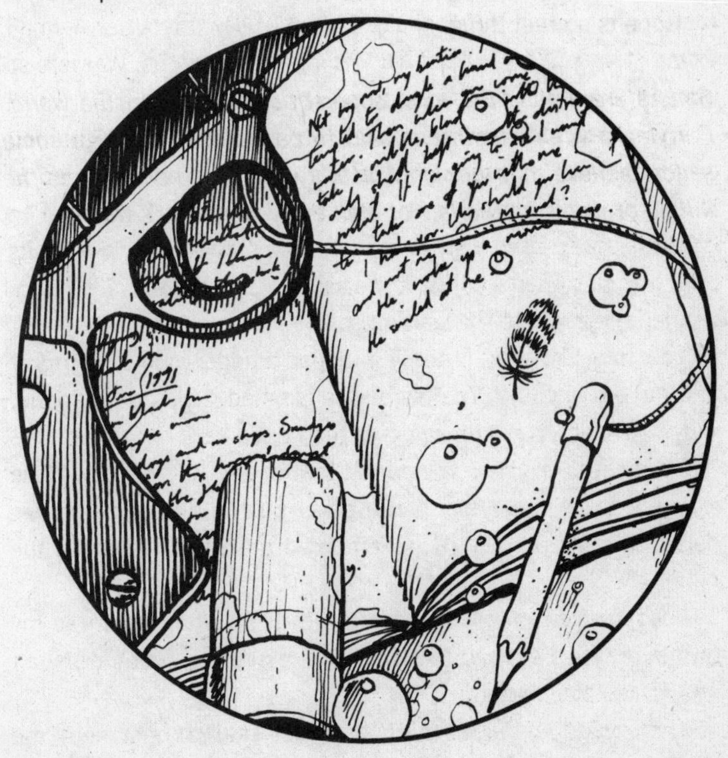

And he is fine. He's a good kid, really. That Maria of his is lucky. So am I. Maybe it's this wren's feather – maybe. I can hold it and look through the porthole at the flat sea.

Flat, blue, calm and empty. Empty except for that black triangle that is following us. I can smile at it now. After all, that shark saved my life. It didn't mean to. It simply got too impatient.

It won't be getting me or my friend. Miguel has invited me to stay with him and Maria when we reach his home port. I'd like that.

That fin is still following us. Hoping that we'll fall into the sea again. Keep hoping, big fish.

Hope is a cruel thing.

Sailors are among the most superstitious people in the world. Carrying a wren's feather is said to be lucky at sea. But some sailors believe that luck only lasts a year. This belief led to the killing of wrens on the Isle of Man every New Year's Day.

FACT FILE

Shark Superstitions and Legends

In the Pacific Islands, where people live with sharks every day, there are many legends and myths.

1. In many parts of Polynesia shark worship is still common.

2. Fortunately, human sacrifices to sharks have stopped. The natives believed that the gods had to have sacrifices to keep them in a good mood. The victim was given only a stick with a shark's tooth on it to defend himself against a shark released into a special pool. Legend says that the best fighters ripped the shark's belly open with the shark's-tooth knife. If that is true, it was a remarkable deed. Most of these gladiators were expected to die. Their death was a sacrifice to the "Queen of the Sharks" who was supposed to live near the bottom of the pool. (On the poor Hawaiian islands a human sacrifice was cheaper than offering the goddess a pig.)

3. The shark-pool of Hawaii was a natural arena made from volcanic rocks. It became the chief harbour of the Hawaiian islands, and was called Pearl Harbor. The American Navy had a base there during the Second World War. They had gathered a huge fleet ready to attack the Japanese as soon as war was declared against them. But Japan struck first and the bombers caught the American fleet in Pearl Harbor. About 2,400 Americans were killed, 1,300 wounded, and 1,000 went missing.

FACT FILE

In that ancient arena of death, humans again proved that they can destroy far more quickly and completely than all the killer sharks in the world. The International Shark Attack File lists all known shark attack deaths since the year 1560. They total just 1,500.

4. A fisherman from the Solomon Islands once explained, "All fish that are in the sea we can eat, but not sharks. Sharks are human. We adore them."

5. Hawaiians tell the story of *mano-kanaka* – sharks that appear in human bodies to make trouble on land.

6. Hawaiian shipbuilders would try to protect their boats by anointing them with the oil from hammerhead sharks. This is still a common custom among some East African boat-builders.

7. Some Pacific Islanders like to catch and eat sharks, and they use the sharks' sense of hearing to attract them. They make rattles from cane and discs of coconut shells, which they dangle in the water.

FACT FILE

8. A traditional Japanese god was a storm-god known as Shark Man. Shark Man was saved from death by a human called Totaro. He made Totaro rich by weeping tears that turned into a thousand rubies.

9. The Indian god Vishnu is sometimes described as coming out of the mouth of a monster fish – probably a shark. Vishnu saved the most precious religious writing in the world when the Earth was flooded.

10. Pearl divers in Sri Lanka protected themselves against attack by paying "shark-charmers" – magicians who could control sharks with spells. They were first written about in 1298 and were still being used in 1866.

THE HORROR OF THE USS INDIANAPOLIS

The word "shark" has come to mean "ruthless " or "cruel". Is that fair on creatures that hunt in order to survive? Are there other creatures in the world that are more cruel and heartless? Look at the story of the worst shark attack ever recorded, and make up your own mind...

The Pacific Ocean off Leyte Island, the Philippines, July 1945

Joel Gauss walked the deck of the ship nervously. "Scared?" his friend, Lieutenant Bob Andrew, asked.

"Aren't you?" Joel asked. "This ship carries death below its decks. " He rubbed his fair, crew-cut hair with a shaking hand.

"But it won't explode," Bob said. "We don't have the bomb on board, you know. We just have uranium-235 down there."

"They say it'll make the most powerful bomb the world has ever seen. An atomic bomb. Just one bomb will wipe out a whole city, "Joel said. "But it needs high explosive to set it off." He waved a hand at the great grey guns. "Hell, Bob, there's enough high explosive here to set off a hundred bombs!"

The ship rolled suddenly and threw the men against a rail. Bob laughed. "Changing course again. Now Captain McVay is scared of something more than a tub of Uranium 235. He's scared of Japanese submarines."

"He has good right," his friend nodded, and looked at the smooth surface of the ocean for any sign of a periscope. "If they knew what we're carrying..."

"But they don't know," Bob said quietly. "Most of the men in this ship don't even know. We're carrying destruction for thousands of Japanese. We've beaten the Germans. With this weapon we'll beat the Japanese too. It'll mean the end of the war, and then we can all go home to our families."

"If the submarines don't get us first," Joel said gloomily.

Bob slapped an arm around his shoulder. "Joel, you are the most miserable son-of-a-gun I ever met. We'll zigzag across the Pacific and we'll reach Tinian Island in one piece. In fact, I'll bet you a dollar we make it!"

Joel shook his head. "If we don't make it I'll be too dead to collect my winnings," he sighed. Then he smiled. "Only joking, Bob."

The two men went to the control room.

Beneath their feet lay the deadliest material known to humans.

Beneath the ship lurked the submarines that wanted to kill them first.

Beneath the submarines swam the hunters that would pick up the pieces when the two enemies tore themselves to pieces.

The sharks couldn't lose.

But the sharks had to wait. *USS Indianapolis* reached Tinian Island safely. It dropped off its cargo, and the scientists set about assembling the bomb that would annihilate a hundred thousand people in Hiroshima. Joel Gauss and Bob Andrew met for their usual chat before they went on duty.

"Not long till the mission's over now, Joel. Not long. Cheer up."

"I'm worried, Bob."

The lieutenant grinned. "Can't remember a time when you weren't worried, Joel, old buddy. What's it this time? We got rid of that bomb, didn't we?"

The other man nodded slowly. "Yes, but that bomb could have saved our lives."

"Saved our lives! Last week you swore it was going to blow us to kingdom come!"

Joel nodded again and rubbed a hand over his hair as he did when he became agitated. "Captain McVay zigzagged across the ocean like crazy to get that uranium-235 to Tinian Island. Do you know why?"

His friend shrugged. "To save our skins."

"No!" Joel Gauss said angrily. "He had orders to protect that uranium at any cost. I've seen the orders for that voyage. If there was a chance that this boat might sink then the first lifeboat had to carry that bomb equipment! They rate it more highly than us."

"No, Joel..."

"Yes, Bob! I drew up the navigation chart for this journey to Japan. We are going straight there, Bob. Straight. No throwing submarines off our trail with some crazy course this time. We're taking the chance that we don't meet an enemy sub because, if we do, he'll be able to follow us as easy as if we put up signposts. We'll all be killed."

Bob Andrew had an answer to that. "You always did look on the black side of things," he muttered.

Beneath the ship the submarine *I-58* waited.

Commander Motchitura Hashimoto could not believe his luck

when he peered into the periscope. A heavy cruiser of the US Navy was steaming straight towards him! It was like a rabbit walking into a hunter's net. Too easy, he smiled to himself.

"Shall we send out a *kaitan*?" his first officer asked.

The *kaitan* was a torpedo guided by a sailor. The sailor could steer the torpedo to make quite sure it hit the target. That sailor would certainly die ... but that didn't matter.

The commander shook his head. "No. No kaitan. Why waste a sailor? This target is too easy. Normal torpedoes will do. Give me a spread of six. Load them now. Fire when I give the order."

It was midnight when the torpedoes hit USS Indianapolis. There was no warning. Many of the sleeping sailors died in the first seconds, as all six shots hit the heavy cruiser.

It sank in twelve minutes.

By some miracle, 850 escaped into the quiet sea. A few life rafts were soon filled. The rest had lifejackets and clung to floating nets. During that first night of confusion 100 of the wounded died.

"Joel!" Bob Andrew cried, as he saw his friend in the water at first light. He dragged himself along the rope that was strung between two boats. "You made it, Joel!"

"I told you we'd be sunk," the Lieutenant shouted.

Bob managed a cheerful grin. "You told us we'd all be killed. Well, I ain't dead yet!"

"And you ain't saved yet," Joel reminded him.

"That submarine will be a hundred miles away by now. Nothing to worry about."

"It's not the submarine that worries me. It's the sharks. The men were talking about them last night," Joel said.

"We'll be rescued in no time. You'll see."

A senior officer stood up in one of the boats and called to the men. His voice carried over the calm sea. "We've not been able to make radio contact with any rescue services," he said. A groan echoed from the men clinging to the nets. "I want you to form in large groups," he ordered.

"That'll make us a better target for the enemy planes, eh?" someone shouted back.

The men laughed nervously. "It'll deter the sharks," the officer cut in. "Sharks won't attack a large group. They search for the weak individuals and pick them off."

The laughter died suddenly and the men hurried to group themselves as the officer ordered.

As the sun rose into the clear sky the first cries came of "Shark!"

"Only a small one. Four foot long at the most," someone shouted. "Don't panic."

Men began to call to the shark, "Here, Whitey! Want to nibble Jim over here – he's so fat he probably won't feel it."

The good humour lasted an hour. Then there was a cry of terror from someone on the outside of a large group. He thrashed at the water briefly before he disappeared.

"Tighter groups!" the officer ordered. The men reorganized themselves, but not an hour went by without the horror of someone being dragged away.

As night fell, the fear grew. Only the sounds and the cries told that the next victim had gone.

For the next three days American planes flew over, but not one spotted the waving men. Fewer men now.

Fewer men, but more sharks. Tiger sharks and white sharks.

"I told you we wouldn't survive," Joel Gauss said.

"You just wait," his friend replied weakly. "Next plane that flies over ... next plane."

"Next plane," Joel said. "Next plane will probably see us.

Bob Andrew looked through his red-rimmed eyes. "Hey, Joel!" he gasped. "Think positive, that's my boy! When *you* start looking on the bright side I just *know* there's a chance for us. Thanks, buddy."

"My pleasure," Joel said, and squinted up towards the sun. He saw it before he heard it. This plane was lower than the others.

This plane didn't fly straight on. This plane began to circle steadily.

It dived low. It was close enough for the survivors to see the airman at the cargo door. As it circled them it threw out all of its own life rafts.

The sailors in the *USS Indianapolis*'s boats were the strongest. Strong enough to paddle after the dropped rafts and drag them back for their comrades in the sea.

There weren't so many crew to fill them now. Of the 850 who

survived the torpedoes' blast and escaped into the water, only 316 were finally picked up.

Some had died of their injuries.

And many had been taken in the most destructive shark attack ever recorded.

No one knows how many of the USS Indianapolis's crew were killed by sharks. Most agree it was at least 100.

No one knows how many died at Hiroshima when the atomic bomb fell – the bomb made from the Indianapolis's cargo. Most agree it was at least 100,000.

And they say sharks are deadly.

The Shark Myths

Sharks do not automatically attack humans when they see them. Even man-eaters have been known to turn tail and flee at the sight of a diver. And when sharks do bother swimmers they "bump" them more often than they bite them.

This action has been experienced many times by swimmers. They feel the shark is trying to drive the humans away rather than kill them. That "bumping" can be very painful – the rough skin is like sandpaper – and the power of the shark's lashing tail can break bones and even kill.

Here are some of the things many modern people believe about sharks. Which of these do you think are true and which false?

1. All sharks attack humans.
False – most sharks are fish-eaters.

2. Shark attacks are fatal.
False – in most shark attacks on humans the human survives. There are about 100 attacks each year. Only about 35 end in the death of the victim.

3. Sharks are hunters, but never hunted.
False – apart from some shark-eating whales, there are sharks that eat other sharks. Dolphins very cleverly gang up to drive away sharks they feel are threatening their young. But sharks'

greatest enemies are humans, who are hunting them almost to extinction. They kill them...

- for sport
- to keep swimming areas safe
- for the leather of their skins
- for the oil in their bodies
- for the protein in their flesh

As a result, some sharks have become endangered species, and killing them has been banned in US waters since 1991.

4. Sharks are the most ferocious fish alive.

False – piranhas live in fresh water and will attack any creature, no matter how large. They attack anything injured or making a disturbance in the water. In 1976, a passenger boat overturned on the Brazilian river Urubu, and 38 Brazilians were turned to skeletons by a single school of piranha fish. Some South American Indians enjoy eating them, but cannot catch them on fishing hooks, because the piranha's razor-sharp teeth will cut through the hook! They have even been reported to leap out of the water and catch low-flying ducks.

5. Sharks attack humans to eat them.

False – most shark attacks are made by a shark trying to protect its home area from human "invaders", just as a guard dog may attack anyone that enters its house.

6. Sharks have pilot fish that lead them to their food.

False – sharks do have "pilot" fish that swim alongside them, but they don't lead the sharks to food – in fact they wait for the shark to kill, then feed off the scraps. The sharks don't enjoy the company of the pilot fish, and it's only the speed of the little fish that keeps them out of the shark's jaws. Sharks have also "stowaway" fish called remoras that attach themselves to the sharks' sides with suckers. But the stowaway is taking a big risk – remoras are often found in the stomachs of sharks.

7. The flesh of hammerhead sharks is poisonous.
False – this is an old legend, but it is not true. The liver of almost any shark is too full of vitamins for humans to eat. The flesh of any shark, including the hammerhead, is perfectly edible. The flesh of sharks caught in the Arctic makes you feel drunk if you eat it raw!

8. Sharks can only breathe by swimming with their mouths open.
False – sharks breathe through gills like other fish. Some sharks do breathe as they swim but they can also pump water through their gills when they are resting, otherwise they would suffocate every time they stopped swimming.

9. A shark will give you an evil wink as it attacks you.
False – sharks don't wink. But they do have a membrane that moves over each eye, and this can give the appearance of a wink.

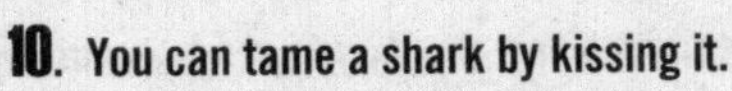

10. You can tame a shark by kissing it.
False – the Fiji Islanders believed that a shark could be tamed by a kiss. Other primitive peoples believed that a human sacrifice to shark gods would keep them happy and keep you safe. Neither method is recommended.

Killers of the Deep

Apart from sharks, there are many other dangers lurking in the oceans of the world.

1. Swordfish

There are cases of humans being attacked by fish that have leapt out of the sea at them. A fisherman from Venezuela called Luis Ramon Flores hooked a swordfish and tried to pull it on board his boat. The fish leapt out of the water and speared him through the forehead. He was lucky to survive. Other monstrous swordfish have attacked boats. In 1981 a 22-metre fishing boat was so badly damaged it had to be towed back to port.

2. Hound fish

Japanese lobster fishermen are more afraid of hound fish than sharks. Hound fish swim at 40 kilometres an hour and can leap five metres out of the water. They are a type of needle fish with pointed noses, and their stab can seriously injure a fisherman. The lanterns on the fishing boats attract the hound fish and a fisherman gets no warning of their rising from the night-blackened sea. An American scientist described how one hound fish leapt at his leg. The needle nose went through his leg and into the deck, pinning him there. Eventually, the fish tore itself free and swam away, leaving the scientist in agony.

3. Stone fish

A nightmare for swimmers is stepping on something sharp, half-hidden in the sand, because it could be a deadly stone fish, which looks like a red and grey rock, and lies in the

FACT FILE

shallow water or tidal pools of the Indian and Pacific Oceans. It has seventeen or eighteen spines on its back, each filled with a deadly poison. The spines are so sharp they can even pierce the sole of a shoe. Its victims may die within hours of being stung.

4. Stingrays

The spines of stingrays are not as poisonous as those of the stone fish, but they can slash the skin of swimmers very badly. Only two or three cases in every thousand end in a human death. In one freak case an army sergeant was swimming in Australia in 1945 when a stingray attacked him. The spines were driven into his heart and killed him instantly.

5. Sea snakes

Many people have a fear of land snakes. They should be more worried by sea snakes. Fifty times more worried! Because some sea snakes have a venom that is 50 times as deadly as that of a king cobra. Their bite is not always painful, but within 24 hours a quarter of all their victims have died.

6. Cone snails

These creatures have such beautiful shells, and are so small, that they look quite harmless. In fact, their pretty exteriors conceal a deadly secret – they have a very clever device for firing poisoned "harpoons" through their noses. Injuries from cone snails are rare, but a quarter of all victims have died.

7. Sea wasps

Sea wasps aren't wasps – they are jellyfish. Their sting is far more deadly than any wasp, and can kill a person in under a minute. They are found off Australian beaches where they kill

F A C T

F I L E

50 people a year – *five times* more victims than sharks in that area.

8. Blue fish

These are the piranhas of the sea. They are found in the Mediterranean and in the Atlantic off the coast of North and South America. Blue fish attack in groups (called "schools"). Although they are small compared to sharks, they are especially vicious. They will struggle out of the water to follow people on to the beaches.

9. Electric eels

If a sea creature doesn't bite you, stab you, sting you or poison you to death, it could give you an electric shock. Electric eels use their electric power to stun their prey or to defend themselves. In a laboratory it can be powerful enough to light an electric bulb. It has never been known to kill a human, however. The Ancient Greek doctor Galen said electric-eel shocks cured headaches. Today most people prefer aspirin.

10. Moby Dick

The story of Moby Dick the whale is fiction ... but based on fact. A gigantic white whale was named Mocha Dick by the whalers who tried to capture him. Between 1819 and 1859 he managed to sink about twenty boats and kill 30 sailors. He used his 35-metre, 110-tonne body to batter ships to splinters, and his tail to create whirlpools that sucked any survivors under. His jaws could crunch lifeboats into matchsticks and harpoons bounced off his thick skin. He was finally caught as he was weakened and dying of old age.

EPILOGUE
THE ELEVENTH MONSTER

And number 11? Of all the creatures that have inhabited the seas there is *one* that could probably be described as the *most dangerous of all.* It has only been around a couple of million years ... and it has only taken to the seas in the last five thousand. Yet it's doing something that 350 million years of natural history couldn't. It is threatening to make that ancient species, the shark, extinct.

Why?

Because it is a creature that doesn't like sharks, and doesn't understand them.

This deadly creature raids the seas, takes what it wants, then returns to the safety of its natural dry land.And it tries to keep its dry land clean by pouring all its wastes into the sea.

What are these creatures? They call themselves "humans".

Two days in history show how unfair these dangerous creatures can often be. On 1 July 1916, an army of humans attacked another army at a place called the Somme in a war called The Great War.

Sixty thousand men died.

The other humans shrugged and said, "Sad, but you have to fight for what you believe in."

The very next day, across the ocean, someone went swimming. He was attacked and killed by a shark.